I0602313

THE CHANGELING TROLL

THE SEATTLE TROLLS TRILOGY: BOOK ONE

LEAH R CUTTER

BOOK VIEW CAFE

The Changeling Troll
The Seattle Trolls Trilogy: Book One
Copyright © 2014 Leah Cutter
All rights reserved
Published by Knotted Road Press
www.KnottedRoadPress.com

ISBN: 978-1-64470-034-1

Cover Art:
ID 21382899 © Prometeus | Depositphoto.com

Cover and interior design copyright © 2019 Knotted Road Press
http://www.KnottedRoadPress.com

Come someplace new…
If you'd like to be notified of new releases, sign up for my newsletter.

I will never spam you or use your email for nefarious purposes. You can also unsubscribe at any time.

http://www.LeahCutter.com/newsletter/

This book is licensed for your personal enjoyment only. All rights reserved. This is a work of fiction. All characters and events portrayed in this book are fictional, and any resemblance to real people or incidents is purely coincidental. This book, or parts thereof, may not be reproduced in any form without permission.

ALSO BY LEAH R CUTTER

Seattle Trolls

The Changeling Troll

The Princess Troll

The Fairy-Bridge Troll

The Troll-Demon War

The Troll-Human War

The Troll-Troll War

The Cassie Stories

Poisoned Pearls

Tainted Waters

Spoiled Harvest

Bloodied Ice

Tanish Empire Trilogy

The Glass Magician

The Desert Heart

The Ghost Dog

The Shadow Wars Trilogy

The Raven and the Dancing Tiger

The Guardian Hound

War Among the Crocodiles

The Clockwork Fairy Kingdom

The Clockwork Fairy Kingdom

The Maker, the Teacher, and the Monster

The Dwarven Wars

The Chronicles of Franklin

Franklin Versus The Popcorn Thief

Franklin Versus The Soul Thief

Franklin Versus The Child Thief

Contemporary Fantasy

Siren's Call

The Immortals' War

Circle of Air

CHAPTER ONE

Christine stood in the doorway to her living room while her younger brother Dennis paced up and down the center of the room. He looked so out of place there, his plaid red-and-green shirt and sloppy jeans standing out against the browns and beiges.

Comforting, solid bookshelves lined the walls of Christine's garden-level apartment. She'd nearly squealed when she'd found them in the basement of the used furniture store. They fit perfectly under the long windows near the ceiling. All her friends were there: Jane Austen and Charlotte Brontë, Clifford Simak and Stanislaw Lem, China Miéville and Clive Kussler, and so many others. Her over-stuffed wing-backed chair sat in the corner, books stacked on tables on either side. The lamp was perfectly placed for optimal light on whatever Christine was reading. A black loveseat was pushed against one wall, piles of books encircling it. A rarely played stereo stood opposite the couch and was also covered in books.

Despite the piles of books everywhere, Christine knew where every single title lay. It was all ordered. Comforting.

But Dennis—he was a ball of nervous energy. Arms wildly gesturing. Complaining. All movement.

Christine tried to pay attention. This was important to her brother. He'd been dumped. Again. Julie? Judy? And he needed something from her. If only he'd get to the point.

"So—you want me to go to this wedding with you?" Christine interrupted.

Dennis turned to Christine, finally stopping, arms akimbo. "You haven't heard a word I've been saying," he accused Christine.

"I have been! You were dumped by…Jane. And you need a date for this event. A wedding," Christine guessed.

Dennis shook his head. "You are unbelievable." He spread his arms wide, taking in her entire living room. "You know why I never come over? Why no one ever comes over? There's no place for anyone else here. There isn't even someplace for other people to sit."

Christine winced. "I can always clean a path to the sofa," she said. The books were merely piled up in front of it, making it difficult to reach. But they weren't piled on top of it. Much. She liked to read there sometimes, on a Saturday, her legs stretched out.

"That's not the point," Dennis said. "At least I'm trying to date and go out and meet people. You're buried here, already, in this tomb. You and your books."

"I know you've never liked this place," Christine said. "But it's my home." She didn't like the open floor-plan of the house Dennis rented. Even their childhood home had always felt barren. All those wide spaces, with just chairs and the odd table to break it up.

Christine's garden-level apartment suited her just fine. The books everywhere. The warm wooden furniture and brightly colored pillows. The cozy bedroom that was a bed, and just a bed, and not much else. The tiny galley kitchen, long and perfect for just one. The old-fashioned claw-foot tub with optional shower. The sense of being enclosed by the earth, safe and warm.

"It's a tomb!" Dennis exclaimed. "You never leave here!"

"I go to work every day in the archives," Christine said. And she didn't always use a delivery service for her groceries, though she did order almost everything else online.

"Another tomb," Dennis sneered.

Other people had called the archives that—just because they were located in a windowless office in the basement of the library. Again, below ground, where Christine felt most comfortable.

But Christine only had to deal with papers, there. Being a librarian had meant far too much contact with people. Being an archivist was so much better.

"You know, I don't have to take this abuse," Christine said. "You didn't have to come over here."

"Yeah, I did," Dennis said. "Mum called. She asked me to."

Christine sighed. "I know. I forgot to call her." She'd missed her weekly call with her mother. She didn't see why she had to do it, except that Mum insisted. There were a lot of social things that Mum wanted Christine to do. That Dennis did, as well. And her dad.

"It isn't just that, Sis," Dennis said. He took two steps closer.

Christine automatically backed up.

"See?" Dennis said.

Christine looked down, ashamed. She didn't like people coming that close to her. She never had. Didn't like to be touched. Always had to be reminded to give her mother and father a hug. To call them and stay in touch. She even had to work at maintaining eye contact with her co-workers.

What was wrong with her?

"Life isn't a chore that you need to finish," Dennis said gently.

"What?" Christine asked. What did he mean by that?

"You should go out. Live a little. I dare you," Dennis said.

"Dare me? Why do you think I'm miserable?" Christine said. "I'm not. I like my life."

Christine heard the lie even as she spoke it. She was comfortable, but even she knew she was missing something. Just drifting. Unfocused. She kept meaning to go back to school. Get a PhD in library science.

But since she had a job—the perfect one, really, that had just fallen into her lap—she didn't ever do much other than work and read.

"I double-dog-dare you," Dennis said. "You should go out tonight."

Christine just shook her head. "I'm happy," she protested.

"Call Mum," Dennis said. He took another step closer.

Christine steeled herself to stay where she was. Her brother wouldn't hurt her. Physically.

"Go out tonight," Dennis urged her. "Go to a bar. Listen to some live music. Mingle. Have a drink. Or three." He reached out gently and touched her elbow. "Live."

Christine sighed. "I am. I do." Going to a loud, crowded bar wasn't really living. She didn't know why Dennis thought it was.

"You know what I mean." Dennis squeezed her elbow and let go of her arm.

Standing this close, Christine realized again just how different she was from the rest of her family. Her mother was British, and her father's family at some point had come from England. Her parents, her brother, and the rest of them all had that fine porcelain skin and rosy cheeks.

Christine's skin was dark, olive-toned. Her eyes were brown, not blue. She was also considerably taller than her brother. Even her father.

It wasn't that there was no family resemblance. She still looked like a Tuckerman. Aunt Edna had even dragged out family photo albums to show her how her bone structure was identical.

However, her coloring marked her as so very different. Her family had also teased her about being the dark-haired Italian cousin.

"Think about it. And plan on coming with me next Friday to Lars' wedding," Dennis said as he turned to go.

"Lars' wedding?" Christine groaned. Lars had been Dennis' best friend in junior high and high school, though they'd lost touch during college. His family was all Swedish, tall and blond.

The first time Lars' mother had met Christine, she'd assumed that Christine was the help, due to her dark coloring. Despite living in Madison Valley, close to Lake Washington, Christine's family hadn't had that much money. It was only Mum's inheritance from a wealthy uncle had let them buy a house outright in the best school district in the city. Their neighbors had all been rich, including Lars. His family vacationed every winter in the Florida Keys and even had a second house in the San Juan Islands.

Lars had teased Christine about being a servant mercilessly, ordering her to go fetch his shoes and bring him pizza. Dennis, of course, had joined in.

Though they'd all grown beyond it, Christine still hated Lars.

"It'll be fun. Promise," Dennis said.

"Do I have to?" Christine complained.

"I promise that I won't let Lars tease you. Too much. Besides, it'll be a good opportunity for you to meet people. Which would get Mum off your back for a while. Me, too," Dennis said.

"Fine," Christine said. "I'll go."

Dennis gave her The Look.

"I promise," Christine said reluctantly. She would never break a promise, particularly not to someone in her family. Dad had taught them there was nothing worse than an oath-breaker.

"Good," Dennis said. "Now, remember the dare, too."

Christine groaned but nodded. She had both a

promise and a dare, now, when all she wanted was to curl back up with her books and forget about the outside world for the rest of the night.

Dennis paused after he opened the door. "You know, I just want you to be happy," he added.

"I know. You have the best of intentions," Christine said. "I just—I don't think your idea of fun matches mine." It never had.

"But have you ever tried?" Dennis asked.

Christine closed the door after Dennis left, the words still echoing in the vestibule.

She *had* tried. But maybe Dennis was right as well. Maybe she should try again. Take his dare. Go to a bar tonight. Listen to some music. Like he'd suggested.

Then she could tell Dennis she'd made the effort. And he'd back down. At least for a while.

How could it hurt?

<hr>

CHRISTINE WALKED UP THE SIDEWALK TOWARD THE bar nearest her home that advertised live music every night. The Seattle night was full of mist, the clouds reflecting back the orange light of the streetlights. The air felt soft against Christine's cheeks and not too cold. They'd had a temperate March so far that year. Crocuses were already blooming. Tulips had started popping their heads out. Trees were budding.

Even from half a block away, the thumping drum from the live performance inside the bar felt like a second heartbeat in Christine's chest. She was certain the main singer wasn't screaming. He must be singing. It was difficult to tell the difference. Three girls stood smoking and giggling next to the building. They all wore similar outfits—the hipster's uniform—skinny jeans, ankle boots, layered tops, jackets and hats.

They gave Christine the stink eye as she passed.

She knew she didn't fit in. Everyone could see that.

She forced herself to keep walking. Up to the door.

The bouncer sat on a stool outside. He wore a black leather biker's jacket. His face was round and white, and his head was shaved. Christine would bet that he worked in an office, probably as an accountant. The closest he'd ever been to a motorcycle was watching a TV commercial for Honda.

"Ten bucks," he said, giving Christine the once-over.

Christine bristled. Ten bucks? She couldn't afford this. She bet the other girls didn't have to pay that much. All they'd have to do was smile and flirt to get in.

But then again, they belonged here.

She wasn't surprised that he didn't card her. She knew she looked older than twenty-eight.

Christine dug into her wallet and pulled out a ten. The bouncer took it. Stamped the back of her hand with something red and toxic, the design smearing instantly.

That was going to take forever to wash out.

The narrow hallway leading to the bar pulsed with sound: the drums, the people, and wailing guitars. Bobbing heads filled the center of the dimly lit room. A large paper dragon hung across the ceiling of the room, swaying with thermals built up by so many bodies.

The band stood on a tiny stage backed into a corner.

The lead singer screamed into the microphone. Even this close Christine couldn't make out the words. The drummer pounded the drums like he was going to war. Arms up over his head then down. Angry and hard. The crowd mostly hid the two other guitarists. One head, then the other, popped in and out of view.

Christine took a deep breath. She just had to endure this for a little while. Then she could go back home. She took off her jacket and slung it over her arm.

Along the right stood a long bar. Lighted shelves ran the length of the wall above it. Chinese lanterns hanging from the ceiling gave off a weird, red glow. A sea of writhing bodies blocked any path to the bar.

How long did she have to stay here to meet Dennis' bet? At least one drink, she decided.

Christine hated having to push her way through the crowd. Like an obstacle course of icky flesh. Plus, she kept zigging when people were zagging, and vice versa. It took forever to get through.

Of course, the bartender wasn't interested in paying attention to Christine. She fished out a bill and waved it, trying to get the girl's attention. Even after the bartender nodded at her, Christine still waited.

The sound of the crowd fought with the band, people laughing and talking. They must all be deaf. At least they looked as though they were having a good time. How did they do it?

Christine tried to observe the people around her without being too obvious about it. Everyone here knew someone else. Maybe that was part of it. Being with friends. The snatches of conversation didn't interest her, though: Who cared who won that singing contest on TV? Had any of them even read a book?

Even in the dim light, Christine could tell she didn't fit. Despite being only twenty-eight, she was still older than most of the kids here. She dressed differently as well, in a loose fitting dark shirt and what Dennis called her mom-jeans, that were very comfortable but fit all the way up to her waist and weren't tight across her butt.

The bartender finally leaned across the bar toward Christine. "What'll you have?" she shouted.

Christine hated beer. She didn't care much for wine either. She'd tried some mead once, at college, and that had been better. Maybe she could just get a coke? "Orange juice," she shouted back eventually. It would be sweet enough, without the caffeine. And bars carried orange juice for their mixed drinks, right? She wasn't about to try for some fancy drink she'd read about.

"You got it."

Christine went back to waiting. She just had to drink her one drink. She didn't have to tell Dennis that it didn't have any alcohol in it. Then she could go home. And she could push it back in Dennis' face that she'd at least tried.

How could anyone find this fun?

At the other end of the long bar, a woman caught Christine's eye. She was blond. As tall as Christine. Her short hair clung close to her head, like a 1920s bob. Christine had always imagined herself in that style, but had never found the courage to try it. The other woman wore a cute brown skirt that went just below her knees. It was the kind of skirt that Christine had always admired but could never get herself to wear. Her white blouse was romantic and looked soft.

When the girl turned and looked to the side, Christine gasped.

Her coloring was identical to the rest of Christine's family—the same porcelain skin as Dennis and her parents.

However, the girl's bone structure was identical to Christine's.

The same tiny nose. The same wide lips. Feature for feature, Christine felt as though she was looking in a mirror. Or an altered photograph of herself.

"Seven fifty," the bartender shouted.

It took Christine a moment to realize the bartender was talking to her. She pushed the ten-dollar bill she had in her hand (more money she couldn't afford to spend) but didn't bother picking up her drink.

Without thinking, Christine took a step, then another, toward the other girl.

Christine didn't know of any cousins living in the city. Was the girl visiting? A tourist? Some other branch of the Tuckerman family that Christine had never met?

That had to be it. The girl belonged in her family. Was a part of her family. Christine recognized her in some deep fashion. Felt a bond with this complete stranger that went bone deep. Like a wizard recognizing her familiar.

Christine had never before wanted to get close to someone, to touch them. Not even in college when she'd made herself try sex for the first time.

But this girl. Christine had to get close to her.

Without thinking, Christine pushed her way past a

boy standing between them. Then through a trio of girls, talking. Christine had to get to the girl before she left.

Finally, the girl noticed something was going on. Her head raised and she grew still.

Unerringly, the girl turned her eyes toward Christine.

Christine had read too many stories about love at first sight to believe it actually happened. And this wasn't like that. There was a shock though. A recognition.

A *spark*.

The girl took a step toward Christine, drawn forward as Christine was being drawn, a force that neither of them could resist.

"No. It isn't possible."

Even in the loud bar, Christine heard the words the girl said.

They were spoken in Christine's voice. Strangers often commented on how it was so deep for a girl.

"You can't be here," the girl announced. "You have to go."

"Why?" Christine demanded. "I have every right to be here. Just like you." How dare this girl. Why was she trying to get rid of Christine? They'd only just seen each other. Just met.

The girl didn't respond. Instead, she put her drink down on the bar (also orange juice) and turned.

She was going to leave.

"No, wait," Christine said.

For the first time in a very long time, Christine reached out to touch someone who wasn't her family. She caught the girl's elbow with her left hand, like Dennis had caught hers earlier.

A shock ran from Christine's fingers, up her palm, then raced along her arm, directly to her heart.

"Ouch!" She let go of the girl and shook her hand.

The girl fled.

Christine stood where she was, unable to move. What the hell had just happened? And why were the lights suddenly so much brighter in the dim room?

It took Christine another few moments to pull herself together and go marching out of the bar. She didn't bother pushing her way past people—for some reason, people now seemed to be stepping out of her way without her having to growl at them.

Outside, the cool night air wrapped around Christine, brushing against her bare forearms, her neck and her cheeks. The hairs all along the back of her neck rose. She hadn't realized how hot it had been in the bar.

Christine looked up and down the sidewalk. All she saw were drunks and smokers, students and kids, really. So involved with their own petty lives. Unaware that something important had just happened.

Where had the other woman gone? It was like she'd just vanished.

But Christine had to find her. There was something about her. Something Christine needed to learn. Something vital.

Christine looked up and down the sidewalk again, but she still didn't see the girl. Somehow, Christine knew she wasn't there. Wasn't anywhere close. Like she'd just hopped in a cab and was already on the other side of town, or stepped in a chimney flue and had been whisked somewhere else.

Despite the stamp on her hand, Christine didn't try to go back into the bar. Instead, she shrugged her jacket on, turned, and started trudging back to her apartment building. At least she'd tried to go out that night. Not even Dennis could fault her for that.

The girl *had* to be related to them. She was a Tuckerman, through and through.

Maybe Mum would know who she was, where she was visiting from. And it would make Mum happy if Christine called without Mum's prompting.

When Christine reached her building, she paused again. It was only a step up from student housing, just about all she could afford. Living here, she didn't have to have a car. Could walk to work. Walk to the grocery store (when she felt like it). Walk to downtown, though she rarely did that.

And because her apartment was in the basement, that just made it more like home. A comfortable place underneath the rest of the building. Christine didn't know why she'd always been drawn to living underground, but that was where her heart was. She loved that warm sense of being enclosed by the earth. Dirt and rocks surrounding her, protecting her from everything outside.

Christine sometimes had odd day-dreams about warrens and tunnels leading off from her apartment, tunneling under the hill. They would be carved out of rock, with beautiful gems still *in situ* in the walls. Rambling and curved, unlike the straight hallways above. Not like a rabbit warren or a hobbit hole. But someplace magical and just hers.

That girl though—she lived above ground. In the light

and air. She was the opposite of Christine in every way. They merely shared features. And something else, something Christine couldn't put her finger on. Some sort of bond that seemed impossible yet still real.

Christine *had to* find her. Somehow.

CHRISTINE WOKE UP WITH HER HEAD POUNDING. THE darkness in her bedroom pulsed in time with her pain. Above the bed, light trickled through the shuttered window. The bedroom was at the back of the apartment, away from the busy front street, so only very soft sounds of traffic sifted through.

The room reeled when Christine made herself sit up. Just past the foot of her bed was a dark rectangle that caught her attention until her eyes finally adjusted.

She'd fallen asleep with her closet door open. Very unlike her. Not because she believed that monsters lived there, as she had when she'd been a kid. She'd outgrown that. She still wouldn't read horror though, not even those young adult novels that were dystopian and so popular. The closed door meant order. Stability. Everything had a place and was in its place.

What had happened to her? Was she getting sick? It wasn't as if she'd gotten drunk at the bar the night before. She'd paid (ten whole dollars!) for a drink she'd never even tasted.

Maybe she was drunk from the noise. She'd felt that before. Punch drunk from too much stimulation. Something no one in her family understood.

Christine inched her way to the edge of the bed. Slid her feet out from the covers. Dangled her toes toward the floor. Were her ankles swollen?

She must be getting sick.

Groaning, Christine pushed herself up to standing. Swayed. Was she going to have to call in to work sick? No. It was Saturday. She'd be well by Monday. She had plenty of sick time saved up, though. She'd never had to call in sick before.

Slowly, Christine dragged herself to the bathroom. She flicked on the switch. The sudden light made her wince.

Looking in the mirror made her wince a second time. Then open her eyes in shock.

It looked as though she'd been punched in the face. Her nose was easily twice the size it normally was. Her skin had always been dark enough that people thought she was perpetually tanned. Now, it was darker. The skin under her eyes was almost black, like it was bruised. Even her lips looked swollen, as if her mouth was growing. Her jaw ached and looked puffy as well.

She touched herself gingerly. Her entire face was tender. Like she had an infection or something.

What the *hell* had happened? Or was happening to her? Should she go to the hospital?

That meant more people. More lights. No. Better to go back to bed. Sleep through it.

Christine went back to bed, pulling the covers up. Over her eyes. Over her head. Nice and dark and warm.

The next thing Christine knew, someone was pounding at her door. *Who? What?* Groggy, Christine dragged herself out of the covers. They tangled her feet, and she wobbled when she stood. Her body felt different. Uncomfortably large. She wiggled her jaw. It didn't fit her head anymore.

"Yes?" she croaked out, ducking into the bathroom to glance at herself in the mirror.

Christine didn't recognize the face that stared out at her. Her brow had come forward, like a Neanderthal's. Her nose had peaked at the bridge, then flattened out, as if she'd broken it in a fight more than once.

But what was worse—Christine's skin had grown darker. And…maybe something was really wrong with her. Because it wasn't just dark. Or brown. It was more olive toned.

Green olive toned.

What was happening to her? Did she want anyone to see her like this?

"It's me," came a familiar voice.

Her voice.

The girl from the bar.

Christine fumbled with the three locks and the chain, finally throwing the door open.

There must be something wrong with her eyes. The girl…*glowed.* Like she had some kind of internal, white fire.

"I'm sorry," the girl said. "I'm so sorry."

"For what?" Christine asked. Even her voice had changed—so much rougher than it ever had been.

"For breaking the spell."

"I'm Christine," the girl announced as she sat down primly on the edge of Christine's love seat. She hadn't seemed bothered by all the books in the living room at all. In fact, she'd found the same path Christine always used, automatically. Soft morning traffic filtered down into the room from the street. The day was overcast, as was typical for Seattle in March. They wouldn't see the sun for at least a couple more months. It was Christine's favorite time of year.

"You have my name?" the original Christine asked. She didn't sit down. She felt as restless as Dennis must have felt the night before, and paced along the only clear path in the living room. Though she kept her steps shorter, smaller, she still felt as though she was lumbering. She was afraid to swing her arms, afraid that she'd knock down her carefully stacked piles of books.

"No, you have mine," the girl said. At Christine's glare, she hastily added, "Let me explain."

"I'm not calling you Christine," Christine told the girl. That was *her* name. The girl already had her face. Or what had been her face. Before she'd gotten sick.

"Well, you can't call me Chrissy," the girl said.

They both winced. Evidently they'd both had bad experiences with that nickname.

"How about Tina?" Christine proposed.

The girl nodded. "That…that's okay." She took a deep breath, let it out. "I don't know where to start."

"Are you a relative?" Christine asked. "A Tuckerman?"

"You could say that," Tina replied. "It's just that I'm the original. You're the changeling. You were matched to me."

"What do you mean?" Christine asked. "A changeling? Like from the myths?" That was almost kind of cool.

Except it meant that she wasn't necessarily human.

"Yes, exactly," Tina said, nodding. She started to glow again. "We were spelled together, bonded magically. So that as I grew older, you'd continue to look identical to me. We're like—sisters. Only different."

Had that been why Christine had never felt right in her body? Because in some ways, it hadn't been hers?

Tina continued to glow brighter. That was also kind of cool. Christine had read about magical light. Often people were enveloped in light when they were about to do magic.

Only Tina wasn't casting any kind of spell. Was she about to explode? Christine didn't like how bright Tina was growing. Like a mini-star, sitting on her couch. She better not leave scorch marks.

"I was taken to be trained in all the magical and mythical pathways. So that I could live up to my full potential," Tina intoned. It was obviously something that she'd been told often. "The Great War is coming. We must be prepared. Or demons and hell-spawn will take over the earth."

"So how do I fit in?" Christine asked. Was she part of this Great War as well?

"You don't," Tina said, her glow diminishing. "You were just a stand-in. A replacement. For me. So that the other side wouldn't realize I'd been taken."

"Oh," Christine said. All the hope stirring in her chest faded. "So I'm not important?"

"You are!" Tina said. "It was very important to fool the other side. So that they didn't realize what was going on."

"So I was just a surrogate for you," Christine said.

Tina nodded sadly. "I'm afraid so."

Part of Christine was relieved. It explained so much, why she never fit in with the rest of her family. Why she'd always felt so awkward around them.

Part of her felt very sad, lost, and alone. Her family, for all its flaws and demands, meant a lot to her.

But it wasn't really hers. Not anymore.

"Then who's my real family? My bio-parents?" Christine asked.

Tina shrugged. "Some trolls."

"Some what?" Christine asked. "Trolls?" Did that mean she was really a troll? That couldn't be right. She also bristled at how casually Tina brushed off her bio-parents. Maybe they weren't important to this Great War, but they were important to *her*.

"Trolls are the most malleable," Tina explained. "So they're often used for changelings. And…" Tina paused, then sighed. "They give up their children for adoption all the time."

"Huh," Christina said. She was going to have to do some research. She did vaguely recall myths about trolls being used to replace human babies, but not something as elaborate as this. And why did trolls give up their children? That didn't feel right, not when Christine thought about how much her family meant to her.

"But you saw me," Tina said accusingly. "In that bar. You *touched* me. You broke the spell."

"You shouldn't have been there in that bar in the first

place," Christine said, stung. How dare Tina say that it was all Christine's fault!

"I just wanted to go out for a night! Have some fun! See what all the fuss was about. Go to a bar and have a drink and listen to music," Tina said wistfully. "I've never been allowed to go. It's been too dangerous. I shouldn't have gone. It's still dangerous. With all the demons. Plus I've always had so much homework. Training and lessons."

"What did you think of the bar?" Christine asked, curious.

Tina shrugged. "Kind of boring. And really hard to hear anyone."

Christine felt a smile tugging at her mouth. *Finally.* Someone else who understood. Then her happiness faded. "What spell were you talking about?" Was that the reason Christine had been so driven to touch Tina? She hadn't felt the same urge since Tina had come into her apartment.

"The changeling spell," Tina said. "The one that hid me from the demons. Kept me safe so that I could learn. The one that made you appear to be human."

"I am human," Christine insisted. She just didn't feel well. She wasn't *transforming.* Despite what the mirror showed.

"No, you're not," Tina said. "Why do you think you live in a basement? I bet you work in one too."

Christine nodded unhappily.

"And you don't feel as though you fit in. You can't stand to touch people. Or have other people touch you," Tina continued.

"What, are you saying I'm some kind of troll? That I've

always been a troll, on the inside?" Christine asked. "And now I'm turning into one on the outside too?" No. This was *not* happening to her.

"Yes," Tina said. "You're reverting back to your natural form. Go take a look in the mirror."

Christine stayed where she was, standing in the middle of the living room for another long moment. Did she really want to see? Maybe this was all a bad dream.

But somehow, she knew it wasn't. She wasn't a troll, or at least, she didn't feel like one. Not on the inside.

What she looked like, however. That was going to be a completely different matter.

Christine turned and walked away from Tina, from that bright *other*. Who had her face and her complexion and would have fit in with her family, more so than Christine ever had.

It was time for Christine to face the music and see what she really looked like. What face was emerging from deep within her. To see if her visage matched the heaviness her body was accumulating.

Time to face the troll.

CHAPTER TWO

CHRISTINE STOOD IN THE DOORWAY TO THE bathroom after she'd flipped on the switch, blinking. Why was the light so much brighter? It glared off the green and gold tile that lined the top half of the walls. The bottom half was wooden wainscoting, which always made the room seem warm. Beige tile with matching gold flecks covered the floor in a decorative diamond pattern. It felt cold under Christine's bare feet.

She didn't look down, though. Didn't look at her arms or hands or toes.

Not until she closed the door and was able to see herself in the full-length mirror hanging on the back of it.

She had…changed. A lot. More than she'd expected. She could see the troll now. Or what a troll must look like. She'd never seen one, actually.

On the one hand, it kind of freaked her out. She no longer looked like herself at all.

On the other hand…it wasn't completely unfamiliar, though she'd never seen this face before.

First of all, there were *fangs*. An upper and lower pair, just starting to push out of her jaw.

Christine ran her finger down to the right canine that prominently hung out over her bottom lip, pushing at the tooth, then at the matching one on the other side. It was real. Not a prop. Not her imagination.

And the points were really sharp. Ow.

How was she supposed to eat with these things? She opened and closed her mouth. Wow. The rest of her teeth had grown jagged as well. It would take one hell of an oral surgeon to fix them. To make them pearly again, and human-straight.

She gave a full-body shudder. She really was turning into something that wasn't fully human, wasn't she?

With an effort, Christine looked past her fangs to the rest of her face, marking the changes.

The ridge across her forehead stood out prominently, making her eyes seem sunken and piglike. Despite how small they seemed, she could still see really well. She'd never needed glasses. Had the pupils changed? They seemed larger, even in the bright light. Maybe that was why it seemed so much brighter in here.

Another ridge had formed across the bridge of Christine's nose. She ran her finger across it. *Bony.* Was it to protect her in battle? Was she going to be getting into lots of fights now?

The bottom of Christine's nose had melted into her face, her nostrils tiny holes. She actually approved of her new nose. It seemed like a good mix of the old and new. She took a deep breath. Despite the size of her new nose, she still felt as though she could breathe normally. And the air seemed to hold more scents, like the smell of toast from the people upstairs, and her own coconut shampoo, and even the light floral perfume that she was certain came from Tina.

Christine looked away from the mirror, down to her hands. The nails were still pink. Well, the nail beds, at any rate. The nails themselves had grown longer, harder, sharper. More like claws. The nails were sharp, like her new fangs. Her hands felt stronger, too. She wasn't going to have problems opening jars of spaghetti, not ever again.

She growled and made a face in the mirror, mimicking clawing at someone. No one would mess with her now. She snorted. They'd probably just run screaming the other direction. She looked kind of like a monster.

She still didn't know how she felt about that.

Christine turned back to the mirror, examining her skin. She didn't know exactly what color she'd use to describe it. It wasn't quite khaki green, that drab olive coloring of military jackets. But it wasn't a forest green either. Something in between. Her skin also felt quite smooth now when she touched it. All the little hairs along her arms had been absorbed. Or had fallen out. Ew. She was going to have to vacuum later.

When Christine dragged a claw (because really, what else was she going to call it?) across her arm, the skin didn't get marked up at all. Didn't show the scratch. Despite how smooth her skin now felt under her fingertips, it had also grown tough as a leather hide.

What other changes could she see? She hadn't suddenly grown tits, which was a shame. She had grown broader shoulders. She could tell from how her shirt wasn't fitting. (She'd really been hoping it had been her chest making her shirt tight.) Her waist hadn't changed, along with her hips or her sex. Her legs were the same, though maybe more muscled, while her feet had grown bigger and longer. The toenails had made the same changes as her fingernails, pink nail beds with longer, claw-like nails.

Christine readjusted her clothes. She still *felt* human. She lifted an arm, sniffed at her armpit. Still smelled the same. And she really needed a shower.

All that had really changed was her face. And her skin. And, okay, maybe her shape had changed a little as well.

Was she really a troll?

Christine peered more closely at her face in the mirror. How were those fangs even useful? Was she supposed to bite people with them? Ugh.

Objectively, Christine knew her new appearance wasn't attractive. Most people would probably find her monstrous, now. She liked some of the changes. The new color of her skin was almost pretty. She liked her nose. But those fangs….

Christine sighed.

The only good thing was that she felt more normal now, whatever normal meant. This body felt good to her.

She knew there would be more changes that she'd discover over the next few days. Her transformation wasn't complete. She didn't feel like this was her body, not yet. It was still something in between.

And she had no idea what she was going to do now. She couldn't go to work this way. Hell, she couldn't even appear in public like this. And what would Mum say?

Who was her mom? And her dad? Did she resemble them, now? What did they do? Where did they live?

Christine hesitated as she reached for the bathroom door. She wanted to stay in the tiny room just a little bit longer. Take some more time to adjust. But she had a guest waiting. Mum would scold her for being a bad hostess. Even if she wasn't really her mum. Even if she didn't know who her family was, or if they'd given her up. They'd still expect her to be hospitable.

After a deep breath, Christine opened the door and walked back out into the living room.

Two creatures had Tina by the arms. They looked like really well-done werewolves—part man, part wolf—except they also looked as though they'd been created out of shadows. Like true monsters, carved out of nightmares. Their matted gray fur was the antithesis to Tina's whiteness, her shine, her glow. While Christine had felt connected to Tina, these two repelled her.

Red eyes glared at Christine from wolf-like faces. Mouths full of fangs bigger than Christine's hissed at her.

"No!" Christine shouted, rushing forward. Her hand automatically formed into a claw. She slashed at the first wolf creature.

Her hand passed through nothing, as if it were merely a shadow.

Tina let forth with a string of words in a language Christine had never heard before. Didn't recognize. Thought she should. The creatures froze.

Christine reached for Tina, grabbed her arm. Tried to pull her free. Slowly started succeeding, breaking Tina loose from the grip of one of the frozen monsters.

Tina's words suddenly cut off. Christine could no longer move her. Tina was as frozen as the creatures. Had the spell backfired? Or been reversed?

The two shadow demons came back to life. They reached for each other. Over Christine's arm. Once their hands touched, a billowing cloud puffed out around them.

Then they were all gone. The demons and Tina. The stench of wet fur remained, choking the back of Christine's throat, foul and unclean.

What had just happened? What were those things? Why had they taken Tina? And where had they taken her?

Christine knew it was all her fault. She'd touched Tina. Broken the spell that made Christine look human.

Tina had said it had also hidden her from the demons.

How could Christine get Tina back? Christine had too many questions. A whole world ripped open before her, with no guide. There was nothing like this in any of her books. Even the internet probably wouldn't be of any help.

Only Tina had the answers Christine needed.

CHRISTINE WAITED IN THE DARKENED BEDROOM while leaving on the light in the vestibule. She could see perfectly fine in the dark, now. She'd checked her pupils again. She'd been disappointed when she'd found that they weren't slitted like a cat's, but still perfectly round.

Dennis should be there any minute. Christine had no idea how she was going to tell him. But calling him was all she could think of. And even though it was early on a Saturday morning, he'd still agreed to come over.

She heard Dennis coming into the apartment building. Recognized his walk. She was really glad that he'd insisted on keys to her place.

Then it occurred to her that that ability was new. Which of her other senses had grown more acute? She was going to have to do some testing later. Look up what was standard human, then determine where she fit on the scale.

Dennis' knock sounded loud in the quiet apartment.

"It's open," Christine called out, aiming for a softer, higher tone. Her voice had been changing too, growing gruffer.

She must have sounded at least a little like herself, because Dennis seemed to recognize her.

"Is this a trap?" he called through the closed door. "Because you never leave your door unlocked."

"I knew you were coming over," Christine said. However, Dennis was right. She never left her door unlocked. She'd have to be doubly careful now, so that no one walked in on her unexpected.

Particularly now that she looked like she did. Now that she was less than human.

"You were the one who insisted on extra locks. Two of them. When you moved in," Dennis pointed out.

"It's just me and it's not a trap," Christine said, exasperated.

"Okay, that sounded more like you," Dennis said. He turned the door handle and walked into the apartment.

"Stay there," Christine told him as he turned toward the living room. He wore his typical Saturday outfit—T-shirt, jacket, jeans, and sneakers. He looked a little worse for wear. Had he gone out drinking last night as well?

"Why? What's going on?" Dennis asked, perplexed.

"I went out. Last night. Like you dared me to," Christine told him.

"Good!" Dennis said. "How did it go?"

"Not like how you expected," Christine warned. "I met someone."

"Really?"

Seriously. How could a twenty-five-year-old man suddenly sound like a thirteen-year-old girl?

"Not like that," Christine said. "I met my twin. A doppelganger." *Your real, human sister.*

"Okay," Dennis said. "And so that's why you're hiding in the bedroom?"

Christine sighed. She was just going to have to show him. Kind of like ripping a Band-Aid off. All at once. "Dennis," she warned. "Now, don't freak out too much. I won't hurt you. This is still me."

She stepped forward, out of the darkened bedroom and into the light.

Dennis frowned. "So this twin made you wear a mask? Did she double-dog dare you as well?"

"It isn't a mask," Christine said. She took another step forward. "This is me. The real me. She's the human. I'm…not."

"Oh, come on," Dennis said. "You're pulling my leg." He stepped closer.

Christine braced herself. She didn't want him touching her. Was that because she was a troll? Tina had seemed to imply that. Or was that just essentially part of her?

Dennis gave a low whistle. "Whoever did your makeup job is a fantastic artist." He peered up at her, then down at her feet. "You're even taller than you normally are, though you're in bare feet. Great hidden lifts."

"It's just me," Christine assured him.

Dennis reached a hand up, then hesitated.

For the first time, Christine reached for his hand, pulled it up to her face. "It's really me. It's not a makeup job."

Dennis pinched her cheek.

"Ow!" Christine managed not to swipe at his hand with her claws, but just barely.

Dennis pulled back for a moment. "What do you mean, this is really you?" His hand reached out suddenly and tugged on her right ear, which now stuck out from her coarse, black hair, pointed and elegant.

Christine had to admit she liked her new ears better than her human ears. She was still trying to see if she could swivel them like a dog's.

When Dennis tried to make a second quick tug, on the other side, Christine blocked her brother's hand. It was just through luck that she didn't break the skin. She did squeeze his wrist, however.

"Ow," Dennis said, pulling back instantly.

Christine let go. "Sorry," she said. She hadn't meant to hurt him.

"I know you haven't been going to the gym," Dennis said slowly. "But somehow, you've grown freakishly strong."

"Did I mention that the other girl—Tina—she's the

human?" Christine asked. "Your actual human sister? That I'm not?"

"Then what are you?" Dennis asked, taking a step back.

"I'm…I'm…I'm a troll," Christine finally admitted. The words echoed and rippled through the apartment, taking on a deep, bell-like tone. Christine felt a huge relief, like an enormous burden had just been lifted off her shoulders.

Dennis shook his head. "I'm not saying I believe you," he said slowly. "But I want to hear the whole story. From the beginning."

"Before you decide to commit me?" Christine asked, amazed at herself that she could joke at a time like this.

Then again, it was just Dennis. And though he technically wasn't her family anymore, he would always be her little brother.

"Sis, you've always been certifiable," Dennis teased back. He stopped. Paused. "This really is you. This really is happening."

"Yes," Christine said.

"Then let's figure out how to fix it," Dennis said confidently.

Christine followed Dennis into the living room, uncertain if "fixing it" was what she wanted.

DENNIS LISTENED CAREFULLY TO CHRISTINE'S TALE— making her tell it twice—before he started asking questions, most of which Christine couldn't answer.

No, she didn't know what the Great War was all about, except that it seemed to involve werewolf-like shadow demons. Two of which had grabbed Tina. Which, thanks to Christine's newly enhanced senses, she could still smell. Ick. No, she had no idea who her bio-parents were. Where they lived. If they'd given her up for adoption or if she'd been stolen (and wasn't that a pretty thought?)

Though Tina had said trolls gave up their children often for adoption, that still didn't sit well with Christine.

When Dennis had finally run out of questions, Christine told him, "I need to go rescue Tina. Those monsters…they weren't right." Christine wasn't certain what they'd do to Tina, but killing her and eating her heart under a full moon came to mind.

Plus, even if they weren't going to hurt her, Christine still had too many questions. And Tina…Tina was her human sister. She'd said they'd been bonded magically. They had a bone-deep connection, like twins did in most of the stories Christine had read.

Christine *had* to find her.

Dennis nodded. "And get her teachers or her family or whoever to put back the changeling spell. So you'll be human again."

Christine cleared her throat. "Dennis—I'm not sure it will be possible to change me back." She hadn't ever really been human, had she? Right now, she felt, if not normal, at least slightly more comfortable than she ever had before. She wasn't used to the double fangs yet. Those would take a while. Or the green tint to her skin. But this body felt a whole lot more like *her*.

"We'll burn that bridge when we come to it," Dennis assured her. "Come on. Let's go see Lars."

"What?" Christine asked, also standing. "Why on earth would we go and see him?" Christine knew he'd been Dennis' best friend and everything. It hadn't occurred to her to try to get some kind of promise from Dennis not to tell anyone.

Dennis shrugged. "Lars knows everybody in Seattle. And if he doesn't personally know about the Great War, he'll know someone who does."

"I can't go out like this!" Christine complained. She no longer looked human at all.

Dennis looked at her critically. "You got a cape?"

"What does that have to do with anything?" Christine asked, perplexed.

"You live on Capitol Hill. In Seattle," Dennis pointed out.

"Central District," Christine said stubbornly.

"All right. Fine. You live in the Central District. You're three blocks from Madison Street, only half a dozen from Broadway. Surrounded by students. Put on a cape and people will just think you're cosplaying," Dennis explained.

Christine opened her mouth to protest, then closed it again. He was probably right. People would probably think her face, her true face, was just a costume.

And she did have a lovely, floor-length purple cape that she bought on impulse. (It had been on sale!) But she'd never had the guts to wear it.

DESPITE HOW CLOUDY AND OVERCAST THE DAY WAS, Christine still found herself squinting. She should have worn her sunglasses. It made sense, really, that if she could see better in the dark, she might not be able to stand sunlight as well. The cool March air felt good against her new skin, though she noticed that it took a much stronger wind for her to feel chilled by it.

And though she wouldn't tell Dennis to his face that he was right, well, he had been right. There weren't that many people on Broadway—it was far too early on a Saturday morning. Most of the places that served brunch wouldn't open until 10 AM. However, nobody ran away screaming when they saw her. A few did seem startled. Those who weren't too involved with their own phones as they walked down the street smiled and nodded at her.

At least one person told her, "Cool costume."

As they walked up Broadway, passing the two restaurants that were open, Christine finally asked, "So where are we meeting Lars?"

"The DIY store," Dennis told her.

"The where?" She'd heard of DIY—do it yourself—before. But there wasn't some kind of craft store, or even a hardware store, on Broadway.

"The Hack Space," Dennis explained. "It's for hackers. And makers. They have a 3-D printer people can rent. Along with a laser cutter. And other tools people can use for making stuff themselves."

"Why on earth would Lars work there?" Christine asked. Really? She'd always imagined Lars would become an investment banker. Something with tons of money attached to it.

Or an IRS auditor. Someone who could ruin other people's lives with a single call.

"He owns the place," Dennis confided in her. "Part of a franchise. It's one of his investment properties. He's putting in a little extra time at this store, just before the wedding, because he'll be gone for a few weeks afterwards. Wants to make sure everything will run smoothly while he's gone."

That made more sense. Because Lars wouldn't have anything to say to real geeks and nerds. They probably didn't even speak the same language.

The store was located in the basement of a building, two currently closed restaurants over it. Both smelled of grease and sweet drinks, making Christine's stomach growl.

As they descended the wide stairs, Christine found herself breathing easier. While she'd always liked being underground, evidently that was something that came natural to her as a troll.

Though the shop had only been open for fifteen minutes, there were already three guys working at the big table in the main room. They all had laptops, tablets, and phones arrayed around them. The wires connecting all the machines formed a complicated net.

Were they playing some game together? Doing some kind of testing? Or were they hacking the Pentagon?

Christine wrinkled her nose at them. They hadn't bathed recently. They all wore either gray hoodies or flannel shirts, with beards of varying lengths.

"Dude!" Lars said, calling out from behind the counter.

He pushed aside the soldering iron and wires that covered the desk so he could reach across and shake Dennis' hand. He stood tall and blond, dressed in a red shirt and black vest. His beard was patchy, but he kept trying.

"Cool cosplay. Are you a she-hulk?" Lars asked, turning toward Christine.

Christine took a deep breath. It had been one thing to show Dennis. It was something completely different to tell this stranger, who wasn't family. Someone she'd known forever, but had never trusted.

"No. I'm Christine," she announced. At Lars' blank look, she added, "Dennis' sister."

"Christine? No way," Lars said, shaking his head, his eyes wide and shocked. He glanced from Dennis to Christine and back again. "You're serious. This is your sister? What, did you lose a bet or something?"

"Sure," Christine said. "A bet and a spell." She knew it had been a bad idea to bring Lars into this.

"It's okay," Dennis said, raising a hand to placate Christine. "Is there someplace we can go to talk?"

"Sure. Come on back here. But I'll have to keep an eye on the place," Lars said. He lifted a corner of the counter so Dennis and Christine could walk behind the desk, into the room that held the laser cutter. It smelled of copper. Small metal shavings covered part of the table that took up most of the space.

Before Dennis could say anything more, Christine asked Lars, "Do you know about the Great War?"

"The war to end all wars? World War I?" Lars asked, confused.

"No. The Great War. That's going on now," Christine said.

Lars looked from Christine to Dennis and back again. Then he gave a long low whistle. "That's really you, isn't it?" he asked. "Not just a great mask and makeup job."

"It really is," Christine said. It was easier this time. To acknowledge that this was her true form.

"I want the full story sometime," Lars said, pointing at Christine. "But I bet that you need information first. Right?"

"Yes," Christine said. The whole world was turning upside down. Lars might actually turn out to be useful.

"I don't know much," Lars said. He steepled his fingers together, then started tapping them rapidly. "I've heard that there's supposed to be this great war coming. Between humanity. And Hell."

After he paused for a long moment, Christine prompted him. "And?"

"That's all I know," Lars said.

"You're lying," Christine said.

"What?" Lars said.

"Christine!" Dennis said at the same time.

Christine shrugged. She'd never trusted Lars. She still didn't.

"Look. Okay. I've heard some rumors. But nothing I know for certain. There was this one really drunk guy one night at a bar—who swore to me, that in the morning, he'd revert back to a pixie—told me that Thomas was the head of the non-human recruits."

"Why would he tell you that?" Christine asked. That

made no sense at all. And it would be just like Lars to only tell her part of the truth.

"Does it matter?" Dennis said hurriedly. "Where would we find Thomas?"

Lars held up his hands. "Now, don't hate me. But this guy swore that he'd be there every night during services."

"Where?" Christine growled.

"Where else? Under the Aurora bridge," Lars said with a smug smile.

Christine blinked for a moment, trying to figure out where he meant. "You *are* kidding me," she finally groaned.

"Nope. Major religious services there. Every night," Lars said.

"In Fremont. Under the bridge. Where the statue of the troll is," Christine said. Why was she not surprised?

"Exactly," Lars replied.

Christine wanted to strike her claws through his smug face, but she controlled herself. "If you're lying, you'll regret it," Christine warned Lars.

"Not lying," Lars said.

Christine didn't believe him. However, she also wasn't sure how to get him to tell the truth. Beating it out of him seemed to be out of the question. He was Dennis' best friend. And she'd always been opposed to violence.

But somehow, that didn't feel as important right now.

She was going to go find this Thomas. Find out more about the Great War. Find out where Tina had been taken.

And come back and deal with Lars later.

On the walk back to Christine's apartment, Dennis agreed to come and pick Christine up later that evening. They'd go visit the Fremont troll under the bridge together.

When they reached the front of Christine's building, Dennis paused and asked, "You sure you going to be okay?"

Christine shrugged. She was tired. And starving. This transforming was exhausting work. But it felt to her as if the changes were almost complete. "I'll be fine," she assured him. "Just—you won't tell Mum or Dad yet. Right?"

"They'll be fine with it," Dennis assured Christine.

"It isn't like I'm coming out as gay or something," Christine told him, exasperated. "I'm *not human*. It's a little different."

Dennis shrugged. "Maybe. Maybe not. But I won't tell them. I'll let you do that the next time you go to visit."

Christine thought about it after Dennis had gone. At least he still treated her like she was family. But what would Mum and Dad say? She didn't think they knew that she was a changeling. Would they love her anyway? Would they still consider her part of the family, even though she wasn't even human? They'd certainly tried to put up with her different nature, though they'd never understood her.

She tried to assure herself that they were still her family, though she wasn't biologically related to them. However, Tina would fit in with them so much better. She looked like them. Was human, like they were.

It was far too easy to imagine Tina taking Christine's place with them.

Between naps, Christine spent the rest of the day looking up trolls on the internet. Not much of it seemed applicable to her. The only thing she found was that it did appear that frequently, troll babies were exchanged for human babies. Her human parents had never been cruel to her, though, so her troll family had never had any reason to come and rescue her.

But why hadn't they come? She felt hurt at that, though she didn't know their circumstances. Did they know she existed? Had they given her up freely, in some kind of adoption process? Or did they think their own girl had died, as a child?

And how could the humans be the good guys here? What kind of good guys would did that kind of thing? Left a family broken that way? It didn't seem right.

Christine also experimented with her strength. She'd grown *much* stronger. It didn't take any effort to turn a wooden spoon into splinters. Her skin was considerably tougher as well. She didn't actually succeed in cutting herself, but she didn't try that hard, either.

It was more difficult to test her hearing. Her ears still couldn't move or swivel, which she considered a serious defect. But maybe she could train herself to do that later.

Teach herself "stupid troll tricks." Like stupid human tricks.

Her sense of taste hadn't changed—spicy things registered the same, along with sweet. What she was hungry for was no longer the same. While a pizza had sounded good, she found herself scraping off all the meat and just eating that. She didn't want a sandwich— all that bread. Ugh. All she wanted was the insides.

Cheese. Meat. Lettuce. Sauce. Even broccoli sounded good.

It didn't take too long for her to figure out how to eat despite the fangs. She just had to be careful not to think about them, or she'd end up knocking her spoon or fork into them at inappropriate times, spilling all over herself.

Typing with just her claws proved to be easy enough, though she might have to resurface her keyboard. Those claws were sharp. But she hadn't lost any dexterity.

By the time Dennis knocked on Christine's door, she felt as though most of the transformation was complete. Her hair had finished turning black. It waved naturally, though it felt coarse to the touch. She was only a smidgen taller, and an equal smidgen wider.

Solid, though. She felt like her feet connected more to the ground than they ever had before, which didn't make any sense. She'd been walking for decades.

Still. It was good to be so connected to the earth. Something she'd never considered before. She'd always liked being in the earth, not walking barefoot through the dirt or something hippish like that. But living underground. Working there.

"Let's go," Dennis said, looking over Christine critically.

"What?" Christine asked. He obviously wanted to say something to her.

"You just seem…comfortable with this. More than I would have thought," Dennis said.

Christine shrugged. "What good would weeping and rending my garments do?" she asked. She still wasn't ready to tell him just how more natural this form felt.

"You *hate* change," Dennis pointed out. "You've stayed in the same apartment for years. Followed the exact same routine, to the letter. But this?"

"It isn't so bad," Christine told him as she slid into the front seat of his car. It didn't have a strong scent, which she appreciated. And being surrounded by metal didn't seem to bother her either—something that many of the internet sites had claimed, that trolls didn't like cold iron.

"Well, don't get too used to it," Dennis warned. "We'll find a way to get you back."

Christine bit her tongue, literally catching it between her sharp, jagged teeth, rather than tell him that she *was* back. Feeling like herself. More than ever before.

CHAPTER THREE

Parking in Fremont was a joke, of course. They ended up finding a spot blocks away from their destination and having to walk back to the monument in the misting rain. A bus of tourists honked at them as they walked. People waved from all the windows, many taking pictures of them.

Christine found that even in her new form her cheeks could grow warm in a blush. She hoped that her green coloring would hide it as well as her darker human skin had.

The orange tinted lights glowed weirdly against the white statue of the troll. In one hand, the troll held a VW bus. Tourists were still getting their photo taken beside it. A hubcap made up one of the troll's eyes. Its steely glare caught the light funny.

Christine looked at the face critically. It was long, with long hair and a big nose. Maybe there was some sort of family resemblance, across the eyes. But it wasn't really troll-like, in her opinion. Where were the fangs?

Before Christine could go closer, a man approached them.

"Brave of you to wear your true face," he said. He had watery blue eyes that looked kind. A very pale, white face. He only came up to about Christine's shoulder, but he was at least twice her girth. Frizzy hair flared out from around his Mariners baseball cap, which added to the illusion of him being just a round ball. He wore a plain blue jacket and jeans.

He looked one hundred percent human.

"What do you mean?" Christine asked, ready to deny it.

"I meant no harm," the man said, raising his hands as if he was giving up. "I wish peace to all creatures. Humans as well," he added, giving Dennis a nod.

"Are you Thomas?" Christine asked, taking a step forward.

It was only then that Christine realized that she'd stepped in front of Dennis, as if to protect him or something. She'd never done something like that before. It was kind of cool how her automatic response was to protect her little brother that way.

"No, no," the man said, shaking his head. "I'm Patrick."

"I'm Christine, and this is Dennis," Christine said, introducing them. She shook Patrick's hand. Though he didn't squeeze her hand inappropriately, she still sensed the hidden strength there.

Was Patrick not human? Was there some other way she could figure that out, without having to touch someone?

"I am very pleased to meet you," Patrick said, nodding. "Have you come to worship?" he asked, indicating the troll with one hand.

"Not tonight," Christine said. Was she supposed to worship the Fremont troll? Was that the religion of her people? There was so much she had to learn! If only she could find some good books, not the fiction that was readily available, or the weird conspiracy blogs on the internet.

"We really needed to find this Thomas," Christine added.

"I'm sorry. I know of no Thomas who comes here," Patrick said.

Christine pressed her lips together so she wouldn't turn to Dennis and say, "I told you so." Lars had been lying. She didn't know why, but she'd never trusted him. Or his family.

"Do you know what race Thomas is?" Patrick asked.

"No, just that he was in charge of the non-human recruits for the Great War," Dennis said.

What were the other races? Were there elves? Fairies? Lars had mentioned a pixie....

"The war," Patrick said with a great sigh. He shook his head. "I'm sorry. I don't believe in violence. I'm a pacifist."

"You are?" Christine asked, curious.

Patrick stood taller and glared at Christine. "Yes. I know, I know. I'm an orc. Whoever heard of an orc who didn't want to get involved in a battle? Didn't want to go out hacking and slashing and grinding the humans' bones into flour for my bread? Who didn't hunger for the rage and the killing and the feel of a sword in my hand…Sorry."

Christine was impressed by Patrick's rant. He obviously still had very strong feelings about the matter.

Patrick visibly pulled himself together. "But I am beyond that now. I practice Zen meditation every day. I work on my breathing, and on being one with the universe. Why can't we all just get along?"

"I don't know," Christine said. She already had her doubt about the human side of things. "The problem is the other side stole someone. Right in front of me. And I need to get her back."

"Who did they steal?" Patrick asked, calm again.

"My…doppelganger. My human sister," Christine said, unsure of how to describe the relationship between herself and Tina without going into the whole story.

"Oh! So you're a changeling. Just come into yourself, eh?" Patrick guessed.

"Yes," Christine admitted. She was relieved as well as disturbed to find out that using troll babies to replace human ones was a common practice.

"Who took your human?" Patrick asked.

"Gray shadow demons," Christine told him. "Looked kind of like wolves. Or werewolves."

"Oh dear," Patrick said. "That's bad. Very, very bad. That the demons came into this world. They shouldn't have done that. It's another break in the DHIVRT treaty." He clicked his tongue several times, rocking back and forth from his heels to his toes, thinking.

"Divert treaty?" Dennis asked.

"Demon-Human Interaction and Visitation Rights," Patrick explained.

"Do you know where I could find these demons? Or how to get her back?" Christine asked. It seemed that Patrick did know something, even if he didn't know Thomas, or believe in the Great War.

"You could pray with us, for her safe return," Patrick said. He glanced over his shoulder to a group that stood in a circle just behind him.

The group was made up of both men and women. Older and younger. White, Asian, and African American. Nobody looked too rich, or like they'd come from Christine's childhood neighborhood and were just slumming it here.

At some point, Christine did want to come back and talk with them.

She turned back to Patrick and shook her head. "No, I don't think that will be enough," she said.

"I didn't think so," Patrick said. "You appear to be a troll of action."

Dennis sniggered. Christine was *so* going to smack him later. It didn't matter if she'd never been full of action before. The situation had never called for it before.

"I can't tell you where the gray demons have taken your friend," Patrick said. "And I can't condone you breaking the DHIVRT treaty, going into their territory, and stealing her back."

"Then what can you do for us?" Dennis asked reasonably.

"In the International District, there's a night market.

You might find your Thomas there," Patrick said slowly. "You'll also find charms there."

"What do charms do?" Christine asked.

Patrick waved in her general direction. "I don't want you to think I'm judging you. However, it might be easier for you if you could, well, sometimes appear human." He gestured to the crowd behind him. "We all have them. I hate having to *pass*, but it is a human's world after all." He finished with a glare at Christine. "And we'd like to keep it that way, thank you very much."

"I don't have any problems with that," Christine said, holding her hands up. Though she had her doubts, given her interactions with Tina, she'd liked growing up human.

"That's what the Great War's all about, you know. At the heart of it. Taking the world away from the humans," Patrick confided.

"Thank you," Christine said. Why couldn't Lars have explained that? He knew more than he was admitting. She was really going to have to talk with Dennis about his choice of friends.

But first, they had to go find something to hide her true self.

WHEN DENNIS PULLED UP INTO THE LOT NEXT TO the International District light rail station, he sat for a moment, not getting out. The rain hadn't gotten any heavier, though Christine wasn't sure if it had gotten colder or not—she didn't appear to feel the cold as much as she used to.

"What?" Christine finally prompted him.

"Do you want to stay in the car?" Dennis asked finally.

"Why would I want to do that?" Christine asked, perplexed.

"Do I need to get you a mirror?" Dennis asked, turning to face her in the dark car.

Christine wondered why he was asking that now. They'd been going out in public together for what felt like all day long. Why would she suddenly change her mind now?

Besides, this was something she had to do. She was the one who had to figure this out. Learn to live with her troll self.

Figure out how to get Tina back.

"I know what I look like," Christine said softly. "But I also know I have to do this."

Dennis drummed his thumbs against the steering wheel of the car. "This isn't the safest place," he finally said. "The International District. Particularly at night."

Christine knew that wasn't what he'd originally intended to tell her. "Don't worry. I'll protect you."

"That wasn't what I meant," Dennis said, still not looking at her.

"Then say what you mean." Christine didn't mean for it to come out as a growl, but it did.

Dennis slowly turned his head to look at her.

Christine felt as though this was the first time he was really seeing her, seeing who she'd become. Actually recognized that she no longer was the human sister he'd grown up with.

But all Dennis said was, "Let's find you a charm, then,

so you'll at least look human. And see if we can find this Thomas. Or any other members of this war. And learn what we can."

Christine got out of the car and followed Dennis. What could she say? He just didn't understand. And she didn't know how to make him understand. He seemed determined to return her to her human form, while Christine was more determined than ever to stay in her current shape.

The night market was held in the plaza in front of the light rail station, as well as along several of the nearby streets. The Chinatown arch was all lit up. It glowed oddly to Christine, like the hubcap eye of the Fremont troll. Stalls lined the sidewalks, lit with their own lights, little havens in between the darkness. The streets were closed to cars. Despite the chilly evening weather, large groups of people walked between the stalls.

Chinese music—high-pitched and scratchy—floated on the air. Underneath that lay the pinging sounds of some sort of game. Christine found her stomach growling in response to the smell of barbecued meat. Normally, she would never eat at this type of street fair. These sorts of things were always so risky. Was her metabolism stronger, now? Since the rest of her was? Could she risk it?

A short man ran out from one of the booths before they'd taken three steps down the street. "You don't want to be going that way," he warned. He had a long nose, almost comically done, hanging down over his broad mouth and whiskers. Bright eyes peered up at Christine from beneath bushy eyebrows. He wore a plain denim jacket and jeans, with a pair black leather biker boots.

"What?" Christine asked, bristling. "What do you mean, we can't go that way?"

"I've known some awfully nice trolls in my time, yes, I have," the man said, nodding his head vigorously. "So I know you don't want to be stirring up anything. What with the troubles we've been having recently."

"What troubles?" Christine asked. Did he mean the Great War? Or something else?

The man paused. Opened his mouth, then closed it again. "Ach. Tourists are ye, eh? We don't get many of your kind traveling through here. No offense, of course."

"None taken," Christine said. Trolls traveled? Well, why not? She knew she wouldn't be traveling much—the thought filled her with dread. But maybe others did.

And being from out of town was certainly a good cover story for her if she didn't want to admit to being a changeling.

"We were interested in some charms," Christine told the man.

"Why didn't you say so in the first place! Do you need to get yours recharged? Or were you looking for something else?" The man gave Dennis the once-over. "Something more exotic for your pet?"

Christine *really* didn't want to know what the man meant by that. "No, no, it's for me," she said hastily before Dennis could say anything. "I need, well, my hiding charm—"

"Say no more, my lady," the man said. He bowed his head to her. "Come with me to Nikolai's Emporium and Trade Goods. I'm sure we can get you fixed up in a jiffy."

"Thank you," Christine said. She hurried after the man, surprised at how fast he moved on his short legs.

"Is it safe?" Dennis whispered in her ear as they approached what appeared to be a derelict apartment building. Cheap plywood boards covered the front windows. Graffiti and handbills covered the wood. At one point, the building had probably been grand. The staircase leading up from the street was wide and made of marble. An ugly wooden door stood where once had probably been leaded glass. There was an alcove to the side. Maybe a doorman had sat there, once, greeting visitors.

Christine shrugged. She wasn't dying to try out her new claws, or to find out how tough her skin was. But she wasn't afraid, either.

"It'll be okay," she whispered back when Dennis seemed to hesitate again.

The short man hopped up the steps. "Nik! Hey, Nik! It's Joey. Got two tourists here. Open up."

Christine chuckled, amused by the change in the man's—Joey's—accent and demeanor. He'd gone from an almost Scottish accent to something that would have sounded at home in the Bronx. They were going to try to hook them, for certain. Was the shop a scam? Were the goods just useless tourist knickknacks?

Then the doorway turned blue and irised open.

Now, Christine hesitated.

"What?" Dennis asked.

"Did you see that?"

"See what?"

"The door," Christine said.

Dennis shrugged. "It just looks like the door opened, to me."

So her eyes had changed as well. What spectrum was she seeing, that would make a doorway glow that rich, deep, blue color?

"Never mind," Christine said, leading the way up the stairs.

If there was something waiting for them up there, they'd have to go through her first before they'd get to her little brother.

STEPPING ACROSS THE GLOWING BLUE THRESHOLD made Christine shiver. *Something* wasn't right with that. They weren't walking through a regular doorway.

Instead of stepping into what she had assumed would be the hallway of the building, they stepped directly into a shop.

Was that blue thing some kind of portal? Where were they now, exactly? Were they inside the same building? Or someplace else entirely?

And how could they get back?

"Don't you worry, Miss," Joey said. "You can walk outta here at any time. Be right back where you were."

"Come on, Dennis," Christine said. She grabbed his arm. He looked surprised, but followed her willingly as she stepped out of the shop, through the portal, back into the darkened International District, then back again to the shop.

"Everything okay?" Dennis asked.

"Seems to be," Christine said, still unsettled by the portal. What did Dennis see? He didn't seem concerned about the doorway at all.

Was it just because it was magic? Or was it something else?

It just made her more determined to find Tina. Get some answers about herself. Her history.

Maybe even about trolls.

"Get a load of this place," Dennis said, looking around. He paused. He seemed much more unsettled by the shop.

The ceilings were tall, shooting maybe eighteen feet up. Christine felt herself standing up straighter. Maybe there were other creatures who were much larger, who also shopped here. Standing wooden shelves, like bookcases, filled the entire space. Many of them looked hand-carved. They came up to her chest. Closer to the front of the shop, they dropped to waist high.

Colorful advertisements covered the walls, mostly in languages Christine couldn't read. Were they even human languages? The ads were for every type of magical thing imaginable. Charms and potions. Lotions to lighten skin, or toughen it. Bags full of glowing items.

Christine looked at the shelves curiously. There seemed to be what she'd consider ingredients, labeled with spidery handwriting, such as rowan twigs and moonwort. Then there was a whole shelf full of purple pouches, with exotic labels like, "Totem of Harmony" and "Disk of Gray."

"Please, please, look around, yes," boomed a jolly voice.

It took Christine a moment to spot the owner. He was

barely three feet tall. He stood motionless at the front of the shop, behind a counter.

He also appeared to be carved out of wood. Lines had been carved into his cheeks to give him age. His nose hung down, long and close to his chin. Bright black painted-on buttons made up his eyes, yet they were still weirdly human. He wore a red-and-white-checked plaid flannel shirt and plain brown pants. His hands were huge but well-articulated, the joints visibly connected with tiny wooden dowels. Yellow straw hung down from under the green knit cap he wore. He was just tall enough to see the tops of the waist-high shelves in the front.

"Hello," Christine said, walking forward slowly. "I need a charm."

"My emporium has the best charms in Seattle," the wooden man boomed. "I'm Nik. What sort of charm are you looking for?" He glanced from Christine and Dennis, curious.

"I need something, well, that changes my appearance," Christine said, fascinated. Nik opened and closed his mouth—it wasn't painted on, though it kind of looked that way. However, his lips didn't move to form any of the words. It was like watching a marionette.

He also wasn't breathing.

"Joey mentioned you were traveling. Did your human transformation charm break?" Nik said.

"Yes," Christine said, guessing that was what Patrick had been referring to.

Nik nodded, then reached below the counter. He brought out three necklaces and laid them on red velvet pillows on the counter.

The simplest was a dark blue stone, about the size of a nickel, wrapped asymmetrically in swooping silver wire. The second had a series of tiny red stones hanging from gold-chain links around a larger red stone set in the center of the piece. The third, if Christine had to guess, was made out of diamonds. Instead of hanging from a chain, the stones encrusted a silver torc that again was asymmetrical, with one loop hanging down in the center while the other end just had a plain silver knob on it.

"Honestly, this one is more my style," Christine said slowly, pointing to the blue and silver necklace.

"Very good, very good," Nik said. "Now, you understand this is an illusion charm, not a transformation charm."

"What's the difference?" Dennis asked, leaning over the counter to look at the three necklaces more carefully.

"An illusion charm just projects the image that you want," Nik said with fond indulgence. He winked one eye at Christine, as if to say, *humans*. It was very disturbing how his button eyes did that. "A transformation charm changes you from one form to the other."

That actually sounded much better to Christine. "My other charm was a transformation charm," she said. "I'd like to try an illusion charm."

"Now, though this charm will enable you to pass ninety-five percent of the time, there are always those races who can see through such illusions," Nik warned. "Dwarves, for example. Masters at seeing through illusions and glamours."

"Thank you," Christine said. There was so much she

didn't know. Maybe Nik had books she could buy, read up on the subject. "How does it work?"

"Do you have an image of the illusion you'd like to project?" Nik asked.

Christine turned to Dennis. "I don't," she said. She hadn't ever liked having her picture taken.

"I think I do," Dennis said, taking out his phone. "Here," he said after a few moments, handing it to Nik. It was from a family gathering—maybe last Thanksgiving. Christine was sitting on the arm of a chair, laughing.

She barely remembered that night—Dennis had kept filling her glass with eggnog that had tasted so sweet. She hadn't realized until the next morning just how much alcohol had been in it.

"Lovely. Just lovely," Nik said. "Now, I can set this illusion into the charm. A single form will take less energy, and you won't have to recharge the charm as often."

"How often will I have to recharge it?" Christine asked. Great. She could just imagine suddenly turning into a troll in the middle of the archives. Or, given her luck, the monthly "all hands" meeting. And how much would it cost?

"That will really depend on you, my dear," Nik said. "If you only wear it during the day, and you don't strain at it, it should last three to four weeks."

"Strain at it?" Dennis asked.

"It has been my experience, in the past," Nik said, "that some races don't take as well to the human form. So they find themselves wanting to appear as their natural shape more often."

Dennis grinned and turned to Christine. "So you're

going to need to not want to *troll-out* too often. Kind of like hulk-out. Get it?"

"Yes, dear," Christine said. "We'll take it."

"Wonderful!" Nik said. "Cash or credit card?" he asked, turning to Dennis.

Christine found herself giving a sigh of relief when Dennis pulled out his wallet. She was going to have to figure out how to pay him back. Someday.

***

CHRISTINE LOOKED AT HERSELF IN THE FULL MIRROR Nik had trundled out into the front of the shop. Her old body looked back. Olive-toned skin, but human, not actually green. Short nails. Short black hair cut in a bob. Dark brown eyes. No fangs. She wiggled her mouth. The fangs were still there. Just—she couldn't see them anymore.

"The charm will grow warm when it's about to wear out," Nik said. "You really won't be able to ignore it."

"Will it also turn red?" Christine asked.

"No, no, we've found that a visual cue doesn't work for most races. Just a physical one." Nik paused. "I like that cape on you. Both of you."

Because the charm was just an illusion, the look of Christine's clothes had changed as well. Nik had warned that a transformation charm would require a change of outfit. "There's always an element of conservation of mass when someone transforms," Nik added. "However, you'll always be more bulky in your native shape."

"Thank you," Christine said again. She felt as though

she could go out and face the world now. Was this what some women felt in terms of makeup? Putting on full war paint?

"Anything else I can help you with?" Nik asked.

As no other customers had come into the shop, Christine took a deep breath and asked, "We were looking for Thomas."

"Thomas?" Nik asked, his wooden features remaining the same. "I don't know of any Thomas. Sorry."

"He's supposed to be the recruiter for the non-humans. For the Great War," Dennis added.

"I thought Hannah was in charge of that," Nik said. He shrugged. "Maybe there's been a change of command, though. You'll find her office down in Pioneer Square." He picked up a pile of business cards off the counter, hurriedly sorted through them, then handed one to Christine.

The center of the card merely said *Hannah Cameron* in a modern script font. The address was printed on the back. No phone number or email.

"A recruitment office?" Christine asked.

"No. She's a lawyer. Keeps regular hours," Nik said. "But are you sure you want to get involved in any of that? You should enjoy your vacation. See the sights. I'm sure you'd love the underground tour."

"Thank you," Christine said. "But we have no choice."

Nik gave a low whistle. It was fascinating really, how he made that sound without pursing his lips. "It's reached all the way to Trollville, eh? Not good. Not good."

Trollville? Was that where most trolls lived? Where was it? How did she get there?

"What's the war about?" Christine asked, coming closer.

"Well, there are three sides to it," Nik said, hopping up onto the counter. "There's the humans, all high and mighty and thinking they know what's best for everyone. No offense," he added hastily, nodding at Dennis.

"None taken," Dennis replied dryly.

"Then there's *kith and kin*, the non-human races. The elves, trolls, dwarves, fairies, pixies, brownies, goblins, orcs, everyone. We lost the last battle. Lost it to the humans." Nik paused, looking thoughtful. "We still just want to be left alone."

"And the third side?" Christine prompted when it appeared Nik wasn't going on.

"Ah. The Host. Angels and devils, demons and cherubs, all the Heaven- and Hell-spawn. Mostly they leave the rest of us alone, too involved in their own squabbles with each other," Nik said.

"Isn't there a treaty?" Christine asked hesitantly. Patrick had said something about that.

Nik rolled his eyes. Absolutely fascinating how he did that, considering they were painted on buttons and didn't really move. "Supposedly. Hell-spawn on one side, not interfering, and Heaven-spawn on the other, also not interfering. Except that they both cross the line. Constantly. Meddling with things that aren't their business. Doing magic in each other's worlds, which is strictly forbidden." Nik shook his head. "The humans aren't much better, I'm afraid. Always sticking their noses in."

"But what do they want?" Christine asked. Patrick had

said it was about taking the world away from the humans. "What's the war about?"

"Greed. Power. The humans won the last round. Of course, the losers aren't always gracious. There's some in the Host who think they should be running the whole shebang." Nik shrugged his wooden shoulders, a very precise move. "I'm not convinced I want the demons running things. Or the angels, for that manner. But neither of them would be bad for business. We sold a lot of charms during the last war. Lots of supplies."

"So you're neutral," Christine said slowly. If there really was going to be a war, she wanted to make sure that Dennis and her family had safer places to be.

"Yes, ma'am. Most shops are. And I'm sure there will be territories, as well as races, who won't join in."

A bell rang behind them. Two smaller creatures, about as tall as Nik, came into the shop. They both were all dressed in brown, brown pointed caps, brown shirts and vests, brown pants, and had little brown clogs on their feet.

Christine would have called them cute, except for their faces. Covered with sores and warts and moles. Odd hairs protruding from them. Deep rivulets carved into their cheeks, around their eyes, even to their chins. Their hands spouted dirty claws, broken and well used.

"If you'll excuse me," Nik said, hopping down from the counter and greeting the new customers with his booming, jolly voice. He spoke a language Christine didn't know. It probably wasn't human, or even based on anything human.

Christine took a deep breath. It was only Saturday

night. This Hannah probably didn't keep hours on a Sunday. Hopefully, as a recruiter, she'd give Christine some time and not charge her anything.

But Lars would still be working tomorrow. At the DIY shop.

"We should go," Christine told Dennis. She knew she'd come back to Nikolai's at some point, if nothing else, for when the charm needed to be recharged. It was friendly and cozy.

If only it sold books.

CHAPTER FOUR

CHRISTINE DIDN'T BOTHER WITH HER CAPE THE NEXT morning. However, she was going to have to invest in new clothes. Her troll body was differently shaped than her human body. Her shoulders were broader. It wasn't as if she'd been in the habit of wearing tight-fitting clothes. Now, only the most baggy things she had would do. She was barely able to squeeze into her jeans—her thighs had grown too muscular. And she appeared to have more hips than before. Shoes no longer fit—she'd gone up at least a size, maybe two.

She wasn't sure how she was going to afford a new wardrobe. Her charmed self showed off everything she wore differently. She'd never realized she had curves before. A shirt that was a little tight on her troll self looked painted on her human self.

Had Nik added a little something to the illusion? She wouldn't have put it past him. Though she grudgingly had to admit that now, she looked kind of how she'd always wanted to.

And what exactly had he been? Animated wood? A creature that had been cursed and turned into a wooden shopkeeper? She had no idea.

Christine had assured Dennis that she would be fine on her own for the day. He had his own things to do, after all. She would call him, though. And she promised she'd remember to do so.

She was actually glad that he'd left her alone for the day. She had her own business to take care of.

Like going and confronting Lars.

The morning was still overcast, but the light seemed softer than it had the previous morning, not stabbing Christine's eyes. She was still warmer than she expected, in a light windbreaker and sweat pants. Her troll body didn't seem to notice the temperature as much as her human one.

Christine felt self-conscious walking down the sidewalk, heading towards Madison. What if her charm suddenly stopped working? She wrapped her fingers around it. It still felt cool to the touch. She hoped that she'd have enough warning, once it got warm, to go and recharge it.

When a young couple holding hands passed the other way, saying, "Morning," Christine jumped. But it was all right. They were just being friendly.

Could she be friendly, now? It wasn't her natural state. She was certain of that.

However, she *was* much more comfortable now.

Maybe she could even try to make some friends.

The DIY shop where Lars worked was empty when

Christine descended into it. Lars was soldering a black transistor onto a green board.

Christine was surprised that Lars knew how to do even that much without burning his fingers. Or burning the shop down. Maybe the shop was more than just an investment opportunity.

Or he was making bombs. That would fit, too.

Lars wore a rust-colored, long-sleeved shirt that day, with a black vest. His black hipster hat sat on the counter beside him.

"So, how's my favorite troll today?" Lars said in greeting.

"Your favorite what?" Christine asked sharply. She thought back to their conversation the previous morning. She hadn't actually mentioned that she was transforming into a troll, had she? Or had Lars just recognized her shape?

"You are still a troll, aren't you?" Lars asked. "Or have you transformed back to human?"

"I knew you weren't telling the truth," Christine said, marching up to the counter. "You know a lot more about the races, *kith and kin*," she accused.

Lars gave her a lazy smile. "Maybe. But I didn't want to freak out your brother."

"Dennis did say that you knew everyone," Christine admitted.

Lars nodded. "Yup. Do."

"So why did you send us on a wild goose chase, looking for a Thomas who doesn't exist? When I should have been looking for a *Hannah* instead?" Christine asked.

She relished her newly righteous anger. She'd never liked Lars.

"I'm surprised you found Hannah," Lars said seriously. "You've been a busy bee."

Christine bit her lip (*softly*) so she wouldn't correct him with *Troll, not bee.*

"What to do, what to do, what to do," Lars said, shaking his head and staring at Christine.

"What do you mean?" Christine asked. She found her spine growing stiffer and she stood up straighter. She wasn't *trolling out* as Dennis would have called it, straining for her natural form.

She was just—wary. Prepared. Practical, really. Given how squirrely Lars normally was. And how mean.

"It really was clever," Lars finally admitted. "What the humans did. Hiding you—I mean your human self—that way."

"Yes, it was," Christine said. "But now, I'd like to find her. That human sister of mine. Take her back from the demons." Particularly if Lars was somehow involved. That would just mean double extra not good.

Lars snorted. "Good luck with that. She has a Destiny, you know."

Christine could hear the capital D in the way Lars said it. "What does that mean?"

"That's something for me to know and for you to never find out," Lars said. "Unless, of course, you decide to join us."

"You're not human, are you?" Christine accused Lars. She *knew* there was something wrong with him, from the first moment she'd met him.

Lars' eyes flashed red. Christine had the impression of great fangs shooting down from his incisors. But he held onto his human form.

"Join us. Haven't the humans screwed up reality long enough?" Lars asked earnestly.

"Who's us, exactly?" Christine asked, wary. Not that she'd ever join a cause that Lars championed. But she needed to learn more. Why weren't there books about this? She'd settle for propaganda pamphlets at this point.

"The Host, of course," Lars said. He straightened up. Though he maintained human form, Christine had the impression of great height.

As well as bat-like, black wings, stretched between bleached bones, that filled the entire room. A shadow creature, just an impression that flashed out of the corner of her eye.

"What would I have to do, exactly, to join you?" Christine asked slowly. She was surprised by Lars' form, hidden under his human skin. Not scared or repelled. It wasn't that she recognized it. But she still felt a kinship, more so than to the humans scattered around them.

"Swear a blood oath to leave your family behind," Lars said immediately. "That they'd be the first to go, if necessary."

Despite the euphemism, Christine knew exactly what Lars was asking for. For her to forsake her human family, as well as her unknown troll relatives, and cleave unto the Host.

The demons.

Would he ask her to kill them? It wouldn't surprise her if he did.

Christine pretended to be considering Lars' offer, hiding her distaste. "And what do I get in return?" she asked.

"You'll be on the winning side, for one," Lars said smugly.

Christine barely stopped herself from rolling her eyes. She was sure they'd said that the last time they'd battled as well, the demons and the humans. "And?"

"Oh, the things I could teach you, my dear," Lars said. "All about yourself. Your magic. I'm sure we could coax greatness out of you."

For once, Christine didn't feel as though Lars was lying. He really did believe he could teach her. That she had potential, no matter how he might feel about her.

Did she have magic? She didn't feel magical.

"I'd like to see Tina, first," Christine said. "See how you treat those you capture. Before I decide." Maybe she could rescue her doppelganger and not actually have to join Lars.

Lars shrugged. "She's merely a human," he said dismissively.

"But according to you, she has a Destiny," Christine pointed out.

Lars thought for a moment before he shook his head. "No. You must swear a blood oath, right here, right now, that you will forsake all others. Join us in our sacred fight. Then you can be shown the secrets."

Christine really wanted to play along with Lars. To take that oath. It would show her where Tina was. Would jump start her training. Would give her an *in* with the other side.

But that was just it. Were they the other side? Or just another side?

And Christine could never break a promise. Let alone a blood oath, whatever that entailed.

"No," Christine said. "Show me Tina first."

"Still a servant to the humans," Lars sneered. "You'll never find her in time. Her Destiny is not unalterable, you know. We can use it. Twist it."

The small room had suddenly grown very warm. Winds swirled around them, pushing the papers off the desk, scattering the small electric solder shavings. The stench of brimstone, like what Christine had smelled with the gray shadow demons, came wafting in.

"You won't win," Christine declared. "I will fight you. I and everyone I can recruit." If for no other reason than to wipe that smug look off Lars' face.

"Please. You can't fight your way out of a paper bag, *troll*," Lars said. "Your people are unprepared. But you could tell them now. To get ready for us. To be ready to kneel before their new masters."

The shadow standing behind Lars grew huge and menacing. Its face was bone white, like a death mask. Its wings were terrible to behold, dripping chaos and darkness.

Christine didn't want to imagine just how horrible Lars would be fully transformed. When he no longer held onto his human shape, and his true self was more than shadow.

"No," Christine said, defying him. "I do not kneel for any man. And you are but a beast."

The charm at Christine's neck blazed hot, scorching her skin. She reached up one hand to touch it.

Lars laughed. The sound chilled the room. Trickled down Christine's spine like ice. "You are already too late. The preparations have begun."

With a final dramatic swirl and a loud bang, Lars disappeared. The winds suddenly died. Christine took a deep breath.

The charm around her neck was cold to the touch, now. Had it suddenly burned out?

Christine turned and caught a look at herself in the reflection of the glass of the door.

For a moment, she saw herself as a troll standing there.

Please, please, please. The charm can't be all used up! It would cost her a lot to get it recharged.

The image wavered. Christine saw herself as a human standing there again.

Would the charm always waver in the face of great heaps of magic? Christine didn't know, but that made sense to her. Magical things always went wonky around each other. At least in most of the books she'd read.

She groaned as she opened the door and left the DIY shop. She'd been right, all these years, about Lars. About how slimy he actually was.

But now, she was going to have to break the news to her brother.

———

"What do you mean, Lars is some sort of demon?" Dennis demanded over the phone.

Christine winced. She was glad she'd called Dennis, and not insisted that he come over and have this conversation in person. She tucked her fuzzy blue blanket more snugly around her legs. At least even in her new form, her living room was comfortably perfect. Snug and underground. Warm and full of books.

"He asked me to swear a blood oath. Forsaking my family. You. As well as my troll family," Christine told him.

"Why would he do that?" Dennis asked.

"Beats me," Christine said. "I don't know why he wanted to recruit me. He never liked me."

"He was my best friend," Dennis mourned.

"I think…I think he was just doing a job," Christine said. "He might have been told to be friends with you. To keep an eye on me." She'd always thought Lars watched her too closely. Not enough to be creepy. But enough for her to always feel self-conscious around him.

"What?" Dennis screeched.

Again, Christine was glad of the miles that separated them. "Tina, my human counterpart? Your actual human sister? Has power. A Destiny." She shivered when she said that. It made her feel so small. Tina had an important part to play. Christine was just a stand-in. "She's magical, remember? They switched us so that she could get her training and come into her full power. Away and out of sight of everyone."

"So he was watching you. To see if you developed powers. So he could, what? Steal you away himself?" Dennis asked. "That almost makes sense. But…he invited me to his house. All the time. If he was just supposed to watch you, he wouldn't have done that. Would he?"

"Dennis, I'm only going to say this once. And deny it later, if you ever ask." Christine took a deep breath. "You're fun to be around. Charming. Delightful sometimes, even. Lars probably did like you in spite of himself."

After an extended silence coming from the other side of the line, Christine asked, "Dennis?"

"Still here. Yeah. Thanks. But it's going to take a while to get over this, you know?"

Christine gave him a troll-like snort. "Tell me about it," she said dryly. "But I think you're doing marvelously well. Better than I would be, if the circumstances had been reversed." Christine wouldn't have been anywhere near as supportive as Dennis had been.

She also would have freaked out a tiny bit more if Dennis had turned into a troll.

Still would, actually.

"So what do we do now?" Dennis asked after another pause.

"We could go back to the Fremont troll tonight. To see Patrick. See if he knows anything more, or could tell us more," Christine said.

"And plan B?" Dennis asked.

"Wait until Monday and talk with Hannah?" Christine said, uncertain.

Dennis gave a long sigh over the phone. "I'm planning on calling in sick Monday morning. I'm assuming you're going to be as well?"

"What? I'm not sick," Christine protested. Being a troll wasn't a disease or something.

"So you can go see Hannah," Dennis said patiently.

"Oh. Okay." Christine paused, then added. "I've never taken a sick day, you know."

Now Dennis snorted with laughter. "I'm well aware. You know, if you would have just gotten out more to start with, we could have avoided this whole mess."

Christine couldn't help herself. She started to giggle, then continued to laugh. "So what you're saying is a few parties and some one-night stands would have done the trick?"

"Exactly!" Dennis said. "But…you know that I support you, right? No matter what form you have."

"Thanks," Christine said. She wrapped her arm around her stomach, giving herself a hug.

Having a younger brother had been such a pain growing up. Particularly one who was as charming and self-confident as Dennis. Having someone who now had her back, though, made it all worthwhile.

FINDING PARKING IN FREMONT ON A SUNDAY NIGHT proved to be just as difficult as it had on the previous night. At least this time, Christine didn't feel so exposed getting out of the car and walking to the troll. Her human illusion was wrapped firmly around her. She felt more human, too, as if she was getting used to the two shapes— the illusion and her true self. The orange-tinted lights still highlighted the white of the troll, and his hubcap eye still had that special shine.

It wasn't difficult to find Patrick and his group. They stood around the VW bus the troll held in one hand, holding candles and singing softly. Christine and Dennis stood to the side and waited until they were finished.

How many in the group were human? They all looked like humans. But were they? Christine wished she had some kind of magical ability so she could see their true forms. Were there elves there? Brownies? More creatures like whatever Nikolai was?

A loud voice startled Christine out of her thoughts. "Come on, now, folks. Time to get a move on."

"Lars?" she said. The human figure appeared to be in a police uniform. But it wasn't strictly human. She could still see that large, winged shadow following it. Would she always see both shapes now?

"You two as well," Lars said, coming up to them, grinning.

Up close, Christine realized Lars wore a security company's uniform. However, it was very close to a police officer's.

"What are you doing here?" Dennis asked Lars. "And why are you wearing that?"

"Wear a lot of hats that you don't know about," Lars admitted to Dennis.

"So you really are…aren't human?" Dennis asked.

Christine's heart ached at how lost her brother sounded.

Lars shrugged. "'Fraid not. No hard feelings, eh? Couldn't just tell you. Wanted to, sometimes."

Dennis nodded slowly. "That's why you have that Shakespeare quote up on your wall, isn't it? The one about there being more to your philosophy, how you always said that related to science."

"That's right, Horatio," Lars said. "Kind of the family motto, actually."

"Wait, so your whole family's composed of demons?" Christine asked. It explained so much about Lars' mom, actually.

"Of course," Lars said. "We wouldn't abandon one of our own. Not like your kind," he sneered at Christine.

"Hey," Dennis said defensively.

"It's okay," Christine said. "I'm used to it." And she was. She'd taken abuse from Lars for years.

Time to give some of it back.

"These are peaceful worshippers," Christine said, stepping forward, into Lars' personal space. Something she'd never done before. She'd always avoided any kind of confrontation with him. "Leave them alone."

"You know nothing of what you're getting involved with," Lars said, drawing himself up.

Christine wished that Dennis could see the change that took over Lars, how white and bone-like his face turned. How menacing his shadow became.

"They're pacifists," Christine said.

"I'm not here to recruit them," Lars told her. "I'm here to break them up. It was given to us, by the LORD, to watch over and herd the lower races."

"Bullshit," Christine told him. "You're a bully, and you're just looking for an excuse to bully someone else."

"He is right," came a timid voice from just behind Christine.

A tiny Asian girl stood there. "It says so in our holiest texts. That as the Angels were created to look over man, so the Demons were created to look over us."

Christine gave a great troll-snort. "Do you know how many times the Bible has been mistranslated? Or given a translation that fit the ruling class better than the original text? Please. Don't believe it. Go back to the original text before you start believing in that crap."

The Asian girl looked thoughtful. "Really? I may have to go look into that," she said, giving Lars a hard look.

"In the meanwhile, you need to go back home, now," Lars said. "Don't want to call the police on you or something."

"We don't want any trouble," Patrick said, coming up. He was still in a plain blue jacket and jeans, though today he had on a Seahawks baseball cap.

Christine bet that in his true form, he was much taller. And more muscular. The reason he was so round as a human was due to the conservation of mass.

"He's just trying to cause trouble," Christine said.

"Well, officer, we'll just be going," Patrick said, bowing his head.

"You don't have to go," Christine told him. "This is public property. And he isn't a real police officer."

"I know that," Patrick said. "But we don't want any trouble," he repeated.

"Can't you at least let them finish their service?" Dennis asked.

Lars gave him a scathing look. "Do you really want to

see what you're defending?" he asked. He pointed a finger at the Asian girl.

With a squeak, the girl's human self melted away. What was left was a creature with bone-white hair, large purple eyes, and fangs. Upper and lower. She had great claws and Christine could see the blood beating in the veins around her eyes, down her neck. She was still Asian, and had an odd beauty to her, for all that she was something from a nightmare.

The girl gasped, then covered herself up with her hands, as if she were suddenly naked. She ran away from the group, up the street, jumping in a car not too far away.

"Not cool, man. Not cool at all," Dennis scolded Lars.

"You're not any fun anymore," Lars complained. Then he folded his arms over his chest and scowled at them. "You should be going too."

"Patrick…" Christine said, turning to him. Maybe they could go to a bar or something? Talk there? But he was already walking away, leading the rest of his congregation.

As they made their way back to the car, Dennis commented, "You know? I never really did like that guy."

Christine cautiously put a hand on her brother's neck, squeezing carefully. She wasn't a hugger. She would never be a hugger. But she knew her brother needed some sort of comfort. It was all she had.

"Thanks, Sis," Dennis said, wearing a brave smile.

And for that smile, Christine knew she'd go into Hell and back.

"Ms. Tuckerman? Ms. Cameron will see you now," said the smooth receptionist. His charcoal suit was perfectly tailored to fit his slim body, his white shirt was so well made it didn't need any starch in the collar, and his power tie was the exact right combination of powder blue and gold.

Christine had fought Dennis all the way to the office, but in the end, he'd let her go by herself. Christine had rightly pointed out that she was going to have to learn how to negotiate this new world without him.

She didn't want to admit that she suspected she'd be more comfortable dealing with her new world without him.

Christine had never been in such a fancy office before. It was a weird combination of comforting and overwhelming. Bookcases lined the walls on either side of the receptionists desk. They rose all the way to the ceiling. The shelves were filled with weighty tomes, encased in red leather with gold printing on the spines. A large window just behind the receptionist overlooked the square itself.

The desk itself was ultramodern and sleek, gray and practical. And empty. What looked like a piece of modern art held up the computer monitor, black and smooth and curved. The chairs in the lobby were uncomfortable pieces of Danish art, in bright oranges and reds. All at odds with the huge wooden timbers holding up the ceiling. The scratched, original, wooden floors.

The receptionist led Christine down a long hallway. Artistic black-and-white photographs lined the walls, all at eye level. Many of them were old-fashioned photos of

Seattle. The seven hills. The old wharfs. A woman's tennis club, with all the players in funny pantaloons and hats.

It turned out that the lawyer's office was clear at the other end of the building, overlooking the Puget Sound. Her office was set up similarly to the front lobby, with huge bookcases filled with important law books, an ultra-modern desk and computer, and the gorgeous view behind her.

Hannah Cameron turned out to be what Christine would call a "horsey-woman." Dishwater blonde hair, straight, that slightly curled under at the ends around her neck and face. A long face with a big nose and square teeth.

Her suit was the most amazing shade of lavender. Not pink. Still a power suit. Was it that particular color? Or the person wearing it?

"Ms. Tuckerman," the lawyer said, standing and reaching over her desk to shake Christine's hand. She was as tall as Christine, possibly taller. Her hands were large and reddened by time outdoors. "I'm very pleased to meet you. What brings you here today?"

Christine had thought a lot about what to say to the lawyer. It all went out the window. "I'm a changeling," she started off with.

"I see," Hannah said, steepling her fingers and sitting back in her chair. "And what brought you to this realization?"

"I met—and touched—my human sister," Christine said. "Then two gray wolf-like shadow demons appeared out of nowhere and stole her away."

"Goddamn it!" Hannah exclaimed. She slapped her

desk hard, pushing herself up. "You see? That's what's wrong with the world today. These demons just think they can invade anyone's home. Anyone's privacy. And just take what they want."

The lawyer made her way from around the desk and started pacing across the floor of her office.

Christine politely swiveled in her chair so as to keep the lawyer in her view.

"We need to stop these senseless attacks. I can slap an injunction on them. Then we can start pursuing damages. How much of your property would you say was damaged?"

"Didn't they violate the DHIVRT treaty by coming into my home in the first place?" Christine asked. She didn't want to get sidetracked into the fact that nothing in her apartment had been damaged.

"Yes, yes, but that will take the court months, if not years, to investigate. There are so many breaches from their side," Hannah said.

"But what about—"

"No, what we really need to do is focus on damages. Bleed the suckers dry," Hannah continued over Christine. "So how much of your property did they trash?"

"They didn't touch my property. They *kidnapped* someone," Christine pointed out.

"Okay," Hannah said, nodding. "So we'll go for half of your property value. Plus psychological damage. Those can really add up."

"But what do I do to get Tina back?" Christine asked, trying to keep her calm.

"Who?" Hannah asked.

"Tina. The human who was kidnapped by the demons. In my apartment," Christine said, barely containing her growl.

"Beh. She's just a human. We don't want to get your rights mixed up with hers," Hannah said, making a dismissive gesture.

"But we need to get Tina back. She's important," Christine said. Why couldn't she get this lawyer to listen?

"I'm sure she's important to you," Hannah said. "But let's not lose track of the big picture here. *Your* rights have been violated. The sanctity of your home destroyed."

Christine tipped her head back and looked up to the tall ceiling, the broad wooden timbers warm against the cool white. "While I appreciate that you're concerned about me, and my rights, I need to find the human who was stolen. First."

"So you don't want to sue the demons?" Hannah asked, puzzled. "I don't see why not. They did hurt you, you know. It may seem minor, but trust me, the violation will creep up on you, make you feel unsafe at odd times."

"I appreciate that," Christine said. "But Tina—she has a Destiny. The other side said that they're going to use it. Twist it."

"Hmmm," Hannah said, slowly walking back around her desk and sitting back down. "I'm not sure that there's any precedent for a stolen Destiny."

Christine managed to contain herself and just issue a soft sigh. "Perhaps, if I could find her and rescue her, we wouldn't have to worry about her Destiny being stolen."

Hannah nodded thoughtfully. "Yes, but then you'd be

breaking the DHIVERT treaty. And I cannot condone an illegal act."

Christine closed her eyes and made herself take a deep breath. The lawyer was in the right. But this had been a tremendous waste of time. Christine opened her eyes and stood slowly.

"Thank you for your time," Christine said. At least the consultation had been free. Christine would have really been angry if she'd had to spend money as well as waste her morning.

Hannah stood and held out her hand. "I'm sorry I couldn't be of more assistance. But if you do decide to press charges, and I think that you should, do keep me in mind."

"I will," Christine said, suspecting that she would never call Hannah. Given how expensive the office was, she doubted she could even afford five minutes of the lawyer's time.

However, the sharp edges of a card were pressed into her palm by Hannah during their handshake. "I wish you the best of luck," Hannah said sincerely.

"Thank you," Christine said, slipping her hand into her pocket and discreetly hiding away the card.

Maybe this hadn't been a complete waste of time after all.

CHAPTER FIVE

CHRISTINE LOCKED THE THREE LOCKS AND SET THE chain on the door behind her automatically. Then she paused, looking at it. Were all of those necessary anymore? Did she really need to be so locked in? There were demons out there. Real ones. Even that shadow image of Lars would give her nightmares, she was sure of it.

However, they also didn't seem to bother with doors, necessarily.

She just felt more confident. More comfortable. Not just because she had more strength, but because this form felt *normal,* despite how jarring it was sometimes to look in the mirror.

The locks stayed. But she wondered, all the same.

Then Christine slipped off her charm, shaking off the illusion of her human body, like a dog shaking off water. Since that first night, the illusion seemed to be stronger, lasting longer after Christine took off the necklace, until Christine made an effort to get rid of it.

Maybe she did need to stay locked away if she didn't

want people stumbling on her when she was in her true form. She put the charm in her pocket, wanting it always to be close by.

In a short while, Dennis came over. Christine handed Dennis the card she'd received from Hannah. It was a very plain, professional looking business card. All it said was, "Ty Brooks—Demon Hunter. Texts Only." And it listed a local number.

"So should I text him?" Christine asked Dennis after telling him about her morning meeting.

"Why not?" Dennis said. "It's probably your first real lead."

"But the expense—" Christine started.

"Maybe he'll take credit cards?" Dennis asked.

Christine glared at him. "I don't use those," she said coldly. Cash was the only thing that satisfied her. If she could pay for everything in cash, including her rent, she would. It was a shame that America had moved away from the gold standard. She'd always dreamed of being able to use bags of gold to pay for things.

"I do," Dennis said.

"You shouldn't have to pay for everything," Christine said. Dennis wasn't debt-free. He had student loan debt, like most people their age. Christine still had at least two years to pay hers off.

"I know. You can pay me back." Dennis paused, then added, "I'm sure we can come up with an equitable arrangement. Like you washing my car or something."

Christine growled at him. "Like hell." She wasn't about to get into some kind of stupid arrangement. Even with her brother.

The brother she'd grown up with. Not that he was her actual brother.

"Let's worry about it later, okay?" Dennis said gently.

Christine would *not* go into debt with her brother. With anyone. But was there any other choice? She needed help. She looked back at the card again, picking up the previous thread. "Of course, Hannah has complete deniability over giving me the card and the number. So if it turns out to be a hoax or something, I can't even accuse her of leading me astray."

"Do you think she was?" Dennis asked.

"I don't know. She was all hot up to go and sue the demons," Christine said. Yet another expense that Christine couldn't afford. "What should I say in the text?"

"Human kidnapped by shadow werewolf demons. Please help!" Dennis suggested.

Christine dutifully started entering in the words.

"No, no," Dennis said. "I was just joking."

"But it's the truth. And that way, we'll know if he's, well, dismissive of humans." Both Hannah and Nik had seemed less than impressed by them. "If he won't work to find them," Christine pointed out, sending the text.

Less than three seconds later, a response arrived.

Thirty Minutes. Five Square Café.

Followed by an address on the north side of downtown Seattle.

"You ready to do this?" Christine asked as she reached in the pocket for her charm. Was she going to wear it out by taking it off and on so much? Would she need an expensive recharge sooner?

"I was born ready," Dennis said in an odd voice.

Christine knew he was quoting from some TV show she'd never seen. "Then let's roll."

———

The café was more like a bar that had been converted into a restaurant. Though people no longer smoked inside, it still had that feel. The bar filled the left side of the room. A half-dozen scattered tables on the other side made the room feel crowded. A bright mirror ran behind the bar, mostly hidden by the bottles in front of it.

Across the back ran a dark, mirror-like surface. It was kind of shiny, but it didn't reflect the occupants of the room at all. However, Christine still found herself distracted by it. As well as by the long hole, just off center, that used to hold a pay phone.

Christine and Dennis had only just sat down when a tall, lanky, African-American man walked in. His long jaw was clean-shaven. Kind brown eyes peered out from under a brown leather conductor's cap. His red T-shirt and jeans jacket rested comfortably over a chest full of muscles. He also wore plain jeans and heavy motorcycle boots. He walked straight over to the table and flopped down on the bench next to Dennis.

"Hey, Ty," called out the waitress from behind the bar.

"The usual, love," Ty called back. "You hungry?" he asked Christine and Dennis.

Christine nodded slowly.

"Times three," Ty told her.

"You got it," the waitress said, scribbling furiously in her pad.

Ty clapped his hands together, once, softly, then rubbed them rapidly. "You guys are in for a treat," he told them.

"Okay," Christine said. She'd noticed her new metabolism had included a great desire for meat and vegetables. Bread of any kind tasted stale. She hoped that whatever "the usual" was, it would turn out to be something she would like.

"I'm Ty," the man said, reaching across the table to shake hands first with Christine, then Dennis, as they introduced themselves.

Was Ty human? He certainly looked human. But there was something about his handshake. Something that reminded Christine of Patrick. That hidden strength. Though his human body looked strong, Christine had the impression that there was much more there than what she could see.

"You got demon problems, huh?" Ty asked, leaning back as the waitress brought all three of them full cups of coffee, as well as a large, steel, banged-up carafe from which they could serve themselves.

"We do," Christine said after the waitress had left.

"Girlfriend?" Ty guessed, turning to Dennis.

"Doppelganger," Christine said. "My...human sister. I guess."

Ty looked at Christine, then turned and deliberately looked in the smoky reflective surface at the end of the room.

For a brief moment, Christine saw the troll form of

herself staring back. Then the illusion charm settled back into place. The reflection darkened. She couldn't see anything again.

"Ah," Ty said. "Changeling?" he guessed.

Christine nodded. Again unsettled that so many human babies seemed to be stolen and replaced with trolls.

At least that confirmed her suspicion. Ty was probably *not* human.

"Well, that puts a whole new spin on things," Ty said, sitting back in his seat. "Why exactly do you want to get her back?"

"She was stolen out of my home. By werewolf shadow demons," Christine explained.

"Okay. So they took her from you. What were you planning on doing to her?" Ty asked, his eyes narrowing, carefully studying Christine.

"I didn't have any *plans* for her," Christine said, aggravated. "I'd just found out. About myself. I was still learning from her. Absorbing what she'd said. She's important to the Great War. She has a Destiny," Christine added.

"And what does that have to do with you?" Ty asked.

"Excuse me?" Christine said, stung.

Ty shrugged. "She got taken out of your home. I get it —that hurts your pride. But why do you want her back? What are your intentions for her?"

"I don't have any intentions," Christine said, frustrated. "I don't want to hurt her. I need her to tell me about my family. About where I come from. Who my bio-parents are."

Ty looked skeptical.

Christine continued. "Plus, it wasn't right that she was taken. She's a human. And she was kidnapped."

Ty still didn't seem impressed.

Finally Christine added, "The demon who told me about her Destiny? I wouldn't mind thwarting him."

"Ah, okay then, we're all copacetic then," Ty said, finally beaming at her. "You see, sometimes a changeling wants revenge. And while I understand and sympathize, I also can't aid in something like that."

"I see," Christine said. When Ty didn't add anything more, she asked, "So does that mean you'll help us?"

"Yes, ma'am," Ty said. "You got yourself a demon hunter."

CHRISTINE SHOOK HER HEAD IN BEWILDERMENT AT all the equipment Ty insisted on bringing into her apartment. First there was a silver metal box that was almost as tall as she was, covered with black dials and gold knobs, even two rows of red and green buttons. Quivering needles hid behind half circles of glass, measuring things Christine couldn't even guess at.

Then came the "sensing array." It looked like a set of stereo speakers. Each had a big black concave circle contained in a wooden box.

Then Ty came back in, carrying yet another huge machine, this time, wearing it on his back. Attached to the side was a spray nozzle. He'd also put on a set of silvery overalls, over his other clothing.

All of it would have fit right in on the set of the *Ghostbusters* movies.

"So where exactly was Tina standing?" Ty asked.

"Right there," Christine said, pointing to the middle of the living room.

"Go stand there," Ty said. "Please."

Christine went and stood where she thought Tina had been. Then she moved three inches over to her right. She saw the demons again in her mind. This was *exactly* where Tina had been standing. When they'd taken her.

"It's okay," Dennis said softly.

Christine realized she'd started growling. Softly. But still. A growl. How dare they?

Ty appeared to take it in stride. First he set up the sensing boxes on either side of her. Then he spritzed something from his spray nozzle onto a plain white handkerchief, testing it. Finally, he walked a slow circle around Christine, spraying every couple of inches. It smelled lemony. She couldn't see it settle into the thick brown carpet. Hopefully it would just evaporate, and not leave a stain or residue.

Next, Ty replaced the nozzle on his spray gun with something that looked like a giant yellow scrub brush. He had to twirl it by hand a few times before it would spin on its own. Then he rubbed it over the carpet as he walked in a circle around Christine.

"Picking up any traces?" Dennis asked after another few moments.

Ty just grunted in response.

Christine shrugged when Dennis looked at her. She didn't have any idea what Ty was doing either.

After circling Christine four more times, Ty walked over to the tall silver machine with all the knobs and dials. He carefully rubbed a small square of white tissue paper around the inside of his nozzle, then fed it into the machine.

The machine started up with a low hum that Christine felt deep in her bones. It wasn't that loud. It just rumbled at the right frequency. The dials on the front wavered wildly, from one end to the other of the spectrum they measured before finally steadying somewhere toward the far right.

Ty turned first one knob, then another. The hum of the machine rose to a hiss. The hairs along Christine's neck stood up.

Maybe the machinery looked like it belonged on a movie set, but it was obviously working and doing *something*.

Now Ty growled, stalking back over to where Christine still stood. He got down on his knees and rubbed at the carpet in front of her feet.

Was he picking up where the beasts had been standing?

Then he repeated the process, feeding the tissue square into the silver machine.

The hiss raised in pitch, becoming a whine.

"Yes!" Ty said. He turned and grinned at Christine and Dennis. "We have a match. I know the ground your demons stepped on just before they appeared here. Chances are, they went back to the exact same place."

Christine blinked, surprised. "You could tell all that?"

"Yes. See the plane balance from where they came

from is different from here. All you have to do is determine the difference in balance between the two planes. It's like…figuring out the PH-balance of your water. And then the balance of the water where the sample was taken."

"I bet it's a little more complicated than that," Dennis said dryly.

Ty laughed. "Oh, it is. But I don't want to bore non-practitioners with the details."

Christine wasn't sure what that meant. Was he talking about other demon hunters? Or something else that they didn't practice? She suspected the latter.

"Want to go have a look-see? See if we can find your Tina?" Ty asked. "They've probably moved on from that place, but I bet I'll be able to track them from there."

"Is it safe?" Christine asked. She glanced at Dennis. While she wasn't really human anymore—and she suspected that neither was Ty—Dennis was.

Ty looked from Christine to Dennis and back. "It's safe enough. We're just going to the Esseuka plains, near the foothills. Not into any of the cities. Or the mountains. He'll be fine."

"I can take care of myself," Dennis said.

Christine nodded. Maybe he could, and maybe he couldn't. But they were dealing with things that were far beyond the experience of either of them. "I'll protect you," Christine promised.

Dennis stared at Christine, then finally laughed softly and shook his head. "You better. Mum would never forgive you if you let anything happen to me."

"I know," Christine said. Particularly since she wasn't really Mum's biological daughter.

"So are we all going?" Ty asked after another moment.

"Please," Christine said.

Finally. They were getting somewhere.

And she was ready to kick any demon's ass who either stood in her way or tried to hurt her brother.

"ARE YOU SURE THAT IT'S SAFE TO DO THAT HERE?" Christine asked Ty again as he sprinkled flour in the shape of a five pointed star on her (clean!) living room carpet. She'd pushed enough books out of the way—against the sofa and into the corner—that he had room to work. All the equipment had been piled together in the vestibule for Ty to pick up later. He'd also slipped out of his full "space suit" so was back in regular clothes.

"You'll be able to vacuum it up later," Dennis said with an exasperated sigh.

"That's not the point," Christine said. Though the way her carpet was being dirtied did, indeed, bother her. "It's just that—by opening a portal here, aren't I making it easier for a demon to come into my apartment?"

Ty stopped what he was doing and looked up at her, puzzled. "You don't have any protection to stop a demon from coming into your place. This isn't making it any easier or harder. If you don't want them coming around, you need to go get some charms or something."

"Oh," Christine said. She hadn't thought of that. Of

course that made sense. "Like what?" she asked, curious. She was already going to have to dig into her savings to pay for everything, like for Ty's fees. Were there any charms she could make herself? Maybe a class in charm making?

Had Lars taught that sort of thing on the side, at the DIY shop?

"Mirrors would be a good place to start," Ty said. He adjusted one of the lines with his boot, rubbing the flour into the carpet.

Christine tried not to notice. Or to growl. "How about a book on charms?" Christine she asked, willing herself to be distracted.

Ty shook his head. "Though English tends to be the *lingua franca* for most of the *kith and kin,* charms and magic usually have to be using the being's native language. And so kids learn it from their parents and teachers. There isn't a huge market for books on magic. Sorry."

Christine sighed. She had so much to learn! Did that mean she'd actually have to find a teacher? She couldn't help the shudder she gave. She'd much rather learn from a book than a person. Maybe it was better to just do without.

"You know those Chinese *ba gua* things? That are eight-sided, bunch of lines on the outside with a mirror in the center? Put one of those up above your door. Demons won't be able to come in that way," Ty added. He got out some different powder and started outlining the star. It smelled like lavender.

Christine nodded. It was good advice, though it didn't appear that demons regularly used doors, not if the pair who had grabbed Tina were indicative of the sorts of things demons regularly did. She was going to have learn all of these things, wasn't she?

How often would they try to break into her place? And would she be able to physically remove them, at least if they were solid?

With a shake, Christine tried to clear her thoughts and relax her hands, which had turned claw-like. She'd noticed her thoughts often turned toward violence these days. Much more than they ever had before.

Ty brought out a long, green bottle and attached a different nozzle, made out of brass with a very fine pointed end. He carefully spritzed the points of each star, then the intersections of the lines. This time, it smelled more like rosemary. Was the scent important? Did it signify the herbs that he used in his concoctions? Or were they just to make it smell nice, to cover up whatever other chemicals he used?

Finally, Ty straightened up. "Ready," he announced.

Christine looked at Dennis. "You don't have to go," she said again.

"Yeah, I kind of do," Dennis replied. "You're my sister, and the only sister I've really known. But this Tina, she's kind of my sister as well." He paused, then grinned. "Besides, don't you think I want to get back at Lars too?"

Christine nodded. She understood that. "I'll protect you," she said. "I promise." With that, Christine took off her charm. Looked at her hands. Still human. Gave a full body shake. Her hands turned green.

Ty watched from the side, a puzzled look on his face. But he merely asked, "Ready?"

"Ready," Christine said. She stepped forward into the

star, standing in the center where Ty indicated. Dennis stood to her right, while Ty took up a spot on her left.

"Let's go kick some demon butt," Dennis said. The three of them held hands, forming a circle between them.

Christine agreed. It was about time that they were finally doing the hunting.

The portal formed up around them. Blue swirling lights shot up from the floor toward the ceiling. Hopefully, it wouldn't leave scorch marks either on the carpet or the ceiling.

Did Dennis see the light? Could he feel how they wavered between one plane and the next, like standing in the doorway of a huge freezer? Hot and cold, solid and not, pink and black, red and gold.

A final wind pushed them the last bit. It felt like stepping into the ocean on a warm, sunny day— shockingly cold despite the warm surroundings. The air turned blue, as if it were thick with cigarette smoke. The smell of sulfur tickled the back of Christine's throat. She recognized that she previously would have wrinkled her nose at the odor. Now, it was almost comforting, reminding her of deep earth and muddy spring rains.

Christine now stood on a rocky plane. The sky was orange, the color of jelly beans, hard, but not sweet. Large gray boulders dotted the hill she now stood on. Nothing green grew here. Gritty red sand pressed against her toes.

Christine coughed and shook her head. Dennis popped up beside her. He looked…smaller here. Smaller than usual. Like he didn't belong. She'd never thought of her brother as frail before. But he was.

She'd promised to protect him, earlier. Now, she

realized she'd have to be extra vigilant. Like how heroes always looked out for their brethren in stories.

Dennis looked up at Christine. He seemed to have to look up higher than usual. His head leaned back all the way, almost resting against his shoulders. "Damn," he said quietly. "You've grown."

"Have I?" Christine asked. She looked at her hands. They seemed normal-sized to her. Then she shrugged her shoulders. She didn't feel any bigger. But her skin felt looser, as if she now had more room for her body to move in.

Ty showed up next. He didn't appear to be fully human after all. He'd kept a human body. Human chest, hands, legs, and feet. However, his face had changed. His nose elongating and his teeth pushing out. It was as if he'd just started the transformation of turning from a human into a dog, then stopped.

"Let's go hunting," Ty said, his voice much deeper and gruffer.

"Lead the way," Christine said. She sniffed the air, but she could only smell the horrid sulfur and dirt of this place.

"Not so fast," came another voice.

Christine turned quickly, claws at the ready.

Lars appeared a little downhill from them. He was fully human, which seemed odd in this place that demanded someone's true form. He wore a typical Seattle hipster's outfit. Skinny jeans tucked into blank ankle boots. A black vest over a dark purple shirt. Emerald green hat, complete with a pheasant's feather tucked into the band on the left side.

"You won't find her, you know," Lars said, striding up the hill, coming closer.

Christine automatically took a step in front of Dennis, ready to protect him. Whatever Lars threw at them, it would have to go through her first before it got to her brother.

"While I'd never admit to knowing anything, whatever or whoever you were seeking isn't here. They left this place, long ago," Lars said, staring hard at Ty.

Christine turned to Ty, who nodded slowly. "Not catching any trace of them," he admitted. "Not the demons or your doppelganger."

"And you are all in violation of the DHIVRT treaty," Lars added cheerfully. "I'm going to have to report you. Get them to pull your license, Ty."

Ty shrugged. "Won't be the first time. Won't be the last."

"I'm sure a judge will be more lenient with you two," Lars said, glancing between Christine and Dennis. "Since it is a first offense."

"And what about you?" Christine asked. "Since we've seen you on earth before. How come that isn't a violation?"

"I keep to my human form at all times," Lars told her seriously.

"You've practiced magic on earth," Christine accused him. Hadn't Nik mentioned that as part of the treaty violations?

"That girl's charm was just about to wear out. She really should have paid more attention to the fading warnings," Lars said sincerely.

Christine didn't bother containing her growl. It echoed loudly across the hill and down into the valley.

"Really?" Lars asked. "Are you really going to challenge me? Here and now?"

"No, no," Ty said, stepping forward and placing a cautious hand on Christine's arm. "She's not."

"I think she just did," Lars said seriously.

"This is the first time she's ever been to a different plane. She's been a troll, what, less than a week? No court would validate your claim," Ty said firmly. "Plus, I'll testify on her behalf. And make sure there's publicity. A *lot* of publicity."

For some reason, that seemed to make Lars back down. Christine wasn't sure why he was so worried about publicity.

"Perhaps you're right," Lars said. "But I suggest you scoot before I change my mind and decide to take her up on it. On the principle of the matter."

"We're going," Ty said. He tugged on Christine's arm. "Come on."

"What about the two demons who came into my apartment? Who took Tina? How do I charge them with the violation of DHIVRT treaty?" Christine asked.

"Do you have proof that they were in your apartment?" Lars asked. "Did they cause damage? Because demons are notoriously ill-mannered when it comes to that sort of thing."

"He found traces of them," Christine said, confident. Maybe she could go after Lars in some legal fashion after all. Not that she could afford it....

"Do the traces still exist?" Lars asked seriously.

"Of course," Christine said.

She felt Ty stiffen beside her.

"Don't they?" she asked, turning toward him.

Ty sighed and shook his head. "Sorry. No."

They all turned. Ty pointed to a glowing spot a dozen yards away. "That's our ticket home," he told them.

"I hope you'll still make the wedding," Lars called after them. "It's going to be the biggest party *ever*."

Dennis paused, then turned, so he was facing Lars again. "You know," he told Lars quietly. "I used to think it was cool. How you bent the rules and such."

"And?" Lars asked, looking bored.

"Now I just know you were being an ass," Dennis told him quietly. "Goodbye, Lars."

Christine was impressed with the finality in Dennis' tone. It wasn't the sharpest, wittiest comeback in the world.

But it was honest. Something Lars had never been.

"I'm sorry," Ty told Christine again as he picked up the final pieces of his equipment from her vestibule.

Christine looked over her shoulder at her still marred carpet. Hopefully it won't take too much to clean it. She couldn't afford to hire a professional cleaning company to come in and do it. "It's all right. You did your best."

"No, I didn't. That's just it," Ty said, turning to her. "I knew they had moved her off. I figured they'd be sloppy, though. I was thinking that she was just this human girl, though, you know? You told me she was special. That she had a Destiny. I should have taken that into account. Started looking elsewhere."

"Like where?" Dennis asked, perking up. While finding Tina was important to Christine, since the conflict with Lars, Dennis had also started taking her kidnapping personally.

"Lars let slip that he was always on earth in human form, right? That he never transforms back to his native shape," Ty said eagerly.

Christine nearly brought up his almost change at the shop the previous day, but it hadn't been an actual transformation. More like a shadow creature, huge and menacing, that the human Lars had worn.

"If he's doing some kind of perversion of the girl, that means he's going to do it *here*. On earth," Ty said.

"Why is that?" Christine asked.

"Tina is human. Her Destiny is here. He wouldn't be able to twist it on some other plane, or in Hell. Not and have it stick. He really has to do it on earth."

"Would it be some big ceremony?" Christine asked.

"Huge," Ty said. "Probably take place at midnight."

"When is Lars supposed to be getting married?" Christine asked Dennis. "And who's the bride?" They had been invited by him, after all.

Dennis shrugged. "I haven't met her. He's getting married this Friday. And the wedding doesn't start until 8 PM. I went to the bachelor party last weekend. Lars had to leave early," Dennis said thoughtfully.

Had he left when Christine had touched Tina? Had that made him alter his plans?

"Oh, this Friday? You mean the thirteenth? When

there's a new moon? Darkest night of the season?" Ty asked.

"Looks like we're going to be crashing a wedding after all," Dennis told Christine.

"I'll need new shoes," Christine told him in return.

CHRISTINE HAD FINISHED HER SHOWER AND GOTTEN dressed for work when someone started pounding on her door.

"Hold on, hold on!" Christine raced from the kitchen into her bedroom to put on her charm. It took a few long moments before the spell activated. Christine breathed a sigh of relief when she looked in the mirror and saw a human standing there again.

Only as Christine started opening the door did she realize that A) she hadn't locked all three locks and B) she had taken the chain off, and was just throwing the door wide open, without verifying who was there.

Then again, as her most recently broken dishes in the kitchen attested, she wasn't really human, either, and was still trying to gauge her own strength.

A young man stood at her door. In his late teens, early twenties. He wore a gray bike messenger uniform with yellow stripes down the sides. A black and red helmet dangled from one arm. He had on short black socks and shoes—never a good combination, especially for someone whose legs were that scrawny.

"Christine Tuckerman?" the guy asked, reading her name from a clipboard.

"Yes, that's me," Christine said. Who was delivering something to her so early on a Tuesday morning?

The man handed Christine a plain brown envelope with just her name on the front.

He waited until Christine had taken the envelope in her hand before he said in a booming voice that echoed weirdly in the hallway, "Christine Tuckerman. You have been served with papers requiring you to appear before the court of the Host on this day of the LORD, at 2 PM."

"*I what?*" Christine asked. She cleared her throat when she realized just how growly she'd sounded.

But the messenger didn't seem put off at all. He replied in a normal-sounding voice. "You have been served, ma'am. I'm just the messenger."

Christine had the feeling he repeated those words a lot.

"But what if I can't make it? I have to work!" Christine complained. The envelope was heavy. The back of it had a red seal. The symbol looked like a pair of wings with a sword underneath.

"Sorry, ma'am," the messenger said, shrugging. He strapped his helmet back on and turned to go.

"You might want to open that inside," he suggested. "Where the neighbors can't see."

"Ah. Okay," Christine said. "Thanks."

She closed the door and sagged against it. What on earth was going to happen when she broke the seal? Opening the envelope wouldn't do anything. The seal on the flap was unimportant. All the magical...whatever... was contained in the wax of the seal.

Had she read that in a book somewhere? She must

have. She didn't really understand magic. Couldn't really sense it. That must be how she understood that breaking the seal was important.

With a huge sigh, Christine put the envelope on the dresser in the vestibule. She did *not* want to call in sick a second day in a row. But she had to tell them something. So she called them, explaining that while she felt better, she had this sudden court appearance she had to make. It was always best to tell at least most of the truth. Then she took off her illusion charm, stuffed it into her pocket, and relaxed back into her natural troll self.

Despite Dennis' assurances, she hadn't been able to fully clean the carpet in the living room. She was going to have to rent a steam cleaner or something. So she took the envelope out there.

Since the carpet there was already a mess, she might as well not damage anywhere else.

Standing in the center of where the five-pointed star had been, Christine cracked the seal. Gasped at the bright light that flowed out from the envelope.

Christine found herself on her butt when an angel (really, there was no other term for the being in front of her, what with the wings and whiteness and all) strode from the envelope and began to speak.

CHAPTER SIX

———

"Seriously, Sis, I've never seen anything like that creature before. Hollywood could take some serious lessons from this guy in how to scare and gross people out," Dennis complained on the phone.

"I wonder why you got sent a demon, and I got sent an angel?" Christine asked. Because they'd both given essentially the exact same message, to get their asses down to the court of the Host by 2 PM.

"You remember that Asian woman? Who said that demons were set to watch over, well, your kind of people?" Dennis said. "Maybe they send the opposite one to mess you up."

Christine didn't have to see Dennis to know he gave a full body shudder. The demon that had appeared to him had scared him. Hadn't threatened him in any way. Hadn't broken anything in his house. Had merely been a completely hairless man with horns, teeth, and tiny wings.

He'd just…moved wrong, according to Dennis. In a

way that was completely inhuman. And that had seriously disturbed Dennis.

Christine hadn't coped much better with the angel. After delivering—her? His? Its?—proclamation, it had disappeared in a poof of lavender smoke. Christine called out after it, "But what if I don't want to?" Like some belligerent two-year-old.

The angel had just set her back up wrong. Maybe Dennis had a point. The messenger was supposed to be unsettling, so they'd hear the message.

Still. She'd felt growly all morning as a result.

"So why don't you come over and we'll take the bus down together to the courthouse?" Christine suggested.

"Parking in your neighborhood is even more impossible than parking downtown," Dennis pointed out. "There will be lots downtown."

"But those cost money," Christine reminded him.

"I can afford it," Dennis said dryly. "How about I just meet you there?"

They didn't really have any idea where the court of the Host was. They both assumed that they'd find access to it at the King County courthouse, in downtown Seattle.

"Fine," Christine said. It wasn't, though. He should be there with her, where she could protect him.

"It will be all right," Dennis said softly. "I know that angel scared you too."

"Not scared," Christine said automatically. And she hadn't been scared. Not exactly.

Just…disturbed. Like Dennis.

They agreed to meet downtown at the courthouse at 1

PM. Neither of them wanted to be late, and they still had no idea where they were supposed to go.

"Would have been convenient if the summons had come with some kind of address attached to it," Christine complained.

"Just because it isn't human doesn't mean it isn't government," Dennis pointed out.

Great. Instead of one governing body, now Christine had to worry about two.

Both of which had the potential to really mess things up, as governments were wont to do.

***

THE BUS DEPOSITED CHRISTINE JUST A FEW BLOCKS away from the courthouse. It was sunny, but cool. Christine was going to have to invest in darker sunglasses. Even more money flying out the door. The other people on the sidewalk appeared to be enjoying the sunny day, smiling and saying, "Good morning," to Christine as they walked by.

Why were people being kinder to her now? Smiling more? Was she smiling more? Or was it just because she felt more comfortable with herself?

Would the court fine her and Dennis for breaking the DHIVRT treaty? Just give them a warning? They wouldn't put them in jail, would they?

And why had the court case been called so quickly? Was it because humans didn't break the treaty as often? Were there four times as many cases of demons breaking the treaty here on Earth, and not so many cases of beings going to the demon lands?

Christine had tried calling Hannah after she'd received the summons, but the lawyer was in court all day that day and unable to take phone calls. She asked for a referral to other legal services, but the two other lawyers she'd called were also in court all day.

It appeared that Tuesday was court day.

Christine waited anxiously outside the courthouse for Dennis. She didn't want to wait inside the building. The lobby was too crowded. She also didn't like the black-and-white murals on the walls. They made the room even smaller. Plus, there was all the security there. Like airport security. Sending her bag through a machine.

When Dennis walked up, Christine breathed a huge sigh of relief. He looked like he was fine, in a white dress shirt, a sports jacket, and slacks. Without thinking, Christine walked straight up to him and reached out a hand to touch his arm.

Dennis pulled back abruptly, avoiding her touch.

"Sorry," Christine said, backing away, ashamed. She'd forgotten that he knew her real identity. That he was human. She wasn't. That he was probably scared of all the *kith and kin*, the Host, everything inhuman, after the visitation this morning.

"No, no, it's okay," Dennis said. He reached out and squeezed Christine's bicep. "I just—I'm still unsettled. You know?"

"Yeah," Christine said. She still wouldn't meet his eye. They started walking back to the courthouse door. "Just needed to make sure you're all right." She didn't need to touch him. It had just been a way of making sure he was okay. She didn't know what she needed, now.

Because he wasn't all right. And neither was she. But did she have the right to ask for anything more? She wasn't really family. Not anymore. Not biologically. Tina was his real sister.

"Sis," Dennis said, stopping in the middle of the sidewalk.

Christine finally looked up. She didn't want to meet his eye. To see the rejection there.

Dennis looked worried. "It really is okay. I just—you startled me."

"No. That wasn't it," Christine said. "It's because I'm *other*. Different. *Kith and kin*. Not human." *Not family.* She managed to not growl at him, though it made her angry. She couldn't help what she was. Any more than he could.

"That *isn't* it," Dennis said through gritted teeth. "You came at me. Fast. Faster than I think you realize. I'm still...freaked. *Anyone* approaching me at any kind of speed would make me step back." Dennis deliberately reached out and tucked Christine's hand into his arm. "Trust me. It isn't you." He paused, then flashed her a grin. "It's me."

"Okay," Christine said, though she wasn't sure she believed him.

She partly understood. She was also still unsettled. More so than she would have thought. Then again, she'd never thought about having an angel give her a proclamation in her living room.

However, discovering that she was a troll hadn't disturbed her as much.

Inside the courthouse, they went through security, stating that they had a summons for 2 PM. Neither Christine's purse or Dennis' wallet beeped as it went through the conveyor belt. The security gates let them through silently. No guards appeared on the other side to hustle them off into windowless rooms.

When they passed through the door on the other side of security, Christine found herself giving a great sigh of relief. She hadn't realized how worried she'd been. That somehow, her troll self would set off alarms or something.

But she kept walking quickly. The narrow hallway leading to the elevators was full of creepy black and white murals. Too busy. Too crowded. Too frantic, like they'd been painted by hyperactive ants.

Past the hallway, they stepped into a large oval area. The floor had beautiful geometric circles of gold and black on either side of yet another creepy mural. The mural was also in gold and black, an old-time scene of Seattle, but falling away into nothingness, as if the city was being dissolved.

Well-polished brass elevator doors lined the area. In between the elevator doors were panels of beautiful black-and-white marble. Elegant lamps hung by chains from the ceiling, giving the area a warm glow. Christine could easily imagine the area in an earlier era, with men and women dressed in suits and long dresses, reflecting the elegance of the building.

At first, Christine and Dennis tried going up the elevators, as high as they could, to see if they could find the court of the Host up there. But though Christine kept her eyes open wide, staring intently, nothing struck her as magical or other. Then they went down into the basement archives, still searching.

No luck.

They tried driving court, immigration court, even went to the child services window.

Nada.

It was drawing close to 2 PM. They found themselves back in the lobby.

"We have to get to the court!" Christine complained. It was like a compulsion. Made her skin itch. They *had* to get there. And on time, too.

"I know!" Dennis said. "Do you see anyone? Who you could ask?"

They'd asked at the information desk already, but the guard had no idea what they were talking about. And it wasn't as if Christine could admit to being inhuman. They'd haul her away.

"The cops are already suspicious of us hanging out so long," Christine whispered. She felt their eyes staring at her back.

Dennis glanced over his shoulder at the uniformed police officer standing in the corner. "I don't think so," he said, bristling.

"What?" Christine said, growing wary. Hands automatically forming claws. Ready to push Dennis out of the way. Was the cop about to draw his gun?

"Your, uhm, illusion body? Dresses in much tighter clothes," Dennis said. He gave her a wry grin, then leaned closer so he could whisper, "He was just checking out your ass."

Christine swallowed hard. No guy ever noticed her before. Mind you, she'd always dressed in loose clothes. Dennis had teased her constantly about being mousy.

A rumbling shook the ground just as 2 PM arrived. "Did you feel that?" Christine asked Dennis.

He nodded. "Felt like a minor earthquake."

But no one else had noticed. The trio of well-dressed (lawyers, Christine guessed) waiting next to them for the next elevator hadn't even glanced up. Neither had the mother with the stroller.

"Dennis," Christine said, clutching at his arm.

"I see," Dennis said.

One of the geometric patterned mosaics in the floor started rotating in a lazy circle. Christine tugged Dennis closer. Pure angelic light spilled from the edges. The gold medallion in the very center of the design irised open.

"Think that's our elevator?" Christine asked, taking a step closer to the mosaic. Then she realized she couldn't have stepped back from it, even if she'd tried. She was being *compelled* to go toward the opening. Just as she'd been compelled that first night to touch Tina.

She growled. She'd never liked being made to do anything.

She liked it even less so, now, as she started coming into her trollhood.

"You know, Sis?" Dennis said, seemingly hypnotized by the opening. "I'm never going to accuse you of not trying new things again."

Stepping into the portal to the court of the Host only reminded Christine superficially of Ty's portal. This one seemed more busy. Plus, it was full of winds that tugged at her shirt, circled around her waist, trickled down her pants.

When Christine arrived at the courtroom, she shook her shoulders and readjusted everything. She suddenly realized what it had been. Some sort of magical pat-down. To make sure she wasn't carrying…something. Wands? More charms? Would guns even work here?

Was she more immune to guns, now? How tough was her troll skin?

The courtroom had what looked like a wooden dormer above the doors set into the far wall. A raised box stood before the door, that a human-looking judge sat in, in formal robes.

To the left of the judge, and a step down, sat three demons, also in robes. They were gray, scaly, and mean looking. One had an extremely long snout, lined with sharp teeth. One was mouthless, just a black hole where the mouth should be. The third had scales for eyes.

They made Christine shudder.

To the right of the judge sat three angels, similarly dressed. They were all human-like, and they had recognizable human faces. The two on the ends were white, while the middle one was African-American. Bright light spilled from them, as if it couldn't be contained. Great shadow wings stirred behind each, fluttering on Heaven's winds.

Another angel, standing on the floor, talked earnestly to the judge. Christine couldn't see the clients, but she assumed they sat at tables in front of the benches that took up the rest of the room.

About half the creatures seated on the benches were human. But only about half. The rest were her kind, non-human, not demon or angel. Most of them Christine couldn't even identify. What was that spiny, hedgehog-looking thing? With bony spurs coming out of the crown of his head and continuing as spikes all down his back? Or the bird-like creature, with the long neck and beak of a pelican?

"Christine and Dennis Tuckerman?" came a whisper from behind them.

Christine turned around. Two beings in identical uniforms stood on either side of the door. One was a dog creature, kind of like Ty, while the other was human.

The dog man motioned for them to come closer. "The court is running a little behind today. Just have a seat. It won't be too long."

"Thank you," Christine said. She and Dennis slid into an empty bench near the back.

The judge and the angel finished conferring. "Step back," the judge announced.

Christine caught odd echoes in his tone. Was the judge actually human? Her gut said no. He just looked that way.

Since when did she have opinions about such things?

"The court finds in favor of the defendant. You can pay the fine to the bailiff. Next up!" the judge called.

No one moved to go to the front of the courtroom.

The judge sighed and stretched to the side, grabbing a large paper calendar. "Alicia McFrabe? Are you present?"

Still no one came forward.

"All right. Since we're already behind, I'm not waiting. Next case. Christine and Dennis Tuckerman."

Again, Christine felt that compulsion to move. She tried not to fight it, but damn it, she was getting tired of that sort of thing.

There had to be a charm or something she could buy, so that she wouldn't have to follow commands like these. Not that she didn't want to show up for court, like Ms. McFrabe. But she had to have some magic to be able to ignore the summons.

Dennis seemed to feel the same need to move. He hurried her out of the bench and crowded close to her as they walked to the front of the court and stood in front of the judge.

Looking up, Christine could tell there was something different about the judge. Something around his eyes. If she cut him, he wouldn't bleed blood. He'd bleed light. Something golden.

"Where is your counsel?" the judge asked, looking down at them.

Christine exchanged a look with Dennis. "How do we get counsel?" Dennis asked.

"First offense, correct?" the judge asked after glancing down at the papers on his desk.

"Yes, sir," Christine said.

"If you're planning on admitting a plea of guilty, you don't really need counsel," the judge assured them.

Both the angels and the demons rustled at that. Were they about to object? But they held their peace.

The judge cleared his throat. "You were found breaking the DHIVRT treaty, in demon lands not by invitation or provision."

"Your honor, there were extenuating circumstances," Christine said, stepping forward. Her heart felt as though it was going to pound out of her chest. She *never* spoke up like this.

But like the other spells, she felt compelled to do so. Not as strongly as a spell. But she had to speak up.

"I'm a changeling," she told the judge, taking another step forward. "I'd just found out. Just started to transform into my native form."

"Troll, right?" the judge asked. He seemed interested.

"Yes, sir. Troll," Christine said. She hoped that wouldn't prejudice him against her. "My doppelganger, my human sister, was stolen out of my apartment by two werewolf shadow demons. I was trying to track them. To find out where she'd been taken to."

"Ah, Ms. Tuckerman, a charge of kidnapping is a very serious matter," the judge said. "I take it you have no proof."

"None," Christine admitted. "But it wasn't right for anyone to just take her that way."

"I see," the judge said. "Have you checked missing persons?"

"No, sir. How would I do that?" Christine asked. Maybe she could use this to her advantage.

"Out the doors, down the hall, to your left," the judge told her. He paused, then looked from her to her brother, studying them both carefully. "You say you've just found out you're a changeling?"

"Yes, sir," Christine said. Maybe they would get off with just a warning. "And this is my brother. He was supporting me, helping me try to find Tina."

"Since there do appear to be additional circumstances, and since you are so new to our world—welcome, by the way—I sentence you to ten hours of community service." The judge banged his gavel. Echoes rippled through the room, like rocks settling after an avalanche.

"But your honor—" Christine protested.

The judge overrode her. "Working *in* the community is a great way for you both to learn about it," he said. "That way, I will never have to see you in my court again. Understood?"

Christine was about to protest more when Dennis reached over and squeezed her elbow. Hard.

"We understand, your honor. Thank you," Dennis said. He tugged at Christine. "Come on."

With a sigh, Christine turned and walked out of the courtroom with Dennis. It wasn't fair. That she was in trouble while no one seemed interested in finding Tina.

When she did find Tina, she might come back to the courthouse. Just so she could watch Tina's kidnappers brought to justice.

At least that made it sound like she had a plan.

———

THE GUARDS AT THE BACK OF THE COURTROOM directed Christine and Dennis to the right. The hall was plain, beige, with what Christine was certain were standard, government-issue beige ceiling tiles and scuffed linoleum floors.

A window was cut into the wall just a few feet up the hall. The wooden shutters were wide open. It didn't take any time for Christine and Dennis to sign up for community service, two hours a week for five weeks. All they had to do was give their email address to a very helpful human clerk. They'd be sent all the instructions they needed, including forms to fill out if they couldn't make their appointed hours.

Then they walked down the hall, past the courtroom, to a set of dark doors with the label "Missing Persons" engraved in gold above them.

Just how many people—creatures—beings—went missing that there was such a large department dedicated to it?

The room beyond the doors looked like a regular government office. No windows. Scuffed white walls made up the room, with cheap dark brown chairs pushed against them. A broad counter separated the waiting room from the rest of the office. Two beings, with pig snouts and tusks to rival Christine's, sat on the chairs, holding each other's hands.

A young man in a red shirt, black tie, and grey vest stood at the desk. He had great blond ram's horns that curled from his temples then around his ears and back up again, framing his cheeks. His nose and face ran long and thin. He had golden eyes with slits for pupils, and concentrated on the computer monitor in front of him. A completely human hand moved a mouse deliberately, as if he were going through a form.

"I'll be with you in just a moment," he said without looking away from the computer as Christine and Dennis approached the desk.

Beyond the man was a typical office. Desks scattered across the room. Papers and computer monitors. People, and others, worked diligently. Overhead, annoying florescent tube lights buzzed. A photocopier clicked away in one corner. Christine smelled coffee and printer toner and someone's too-sweet perfume.

"There," the man at the counter said, with a final click. He turned and smiled at them. "Paperwork," he said with a wry grin.

It seemed to be a universal constant.

"How can I help you?" he asked.

"We're here to see if someone has filed a missing persons report," Dennis said.

"Okay," the man said slowly. "You're not here to file one yourselves?"

"I don't think we have enough information to do that," Christine admitted. "I mean, I know the girl's first name. But not her last."

"And why do you think she's missing?" the man behind the counter asked. His demeanor had grown more stiff and formal.

"She was kidnapped from my living room," Christine told him. "By two demons."

"Ah," the man said nodding and seeming to relax. "There probably isn't a report, then."

"Why not?" Christine asked. Why wouldn't someone report Tina missing? Particularly if she was so important?

"What did this girl look like?" the man asked.

"Like me," Christine admitted. "Except lighter. More blond."

"A changeling!" the man said, surprised. "I see. They still might not have reported her as missing. They wouldn't want to alert people who shouldn't know that she was gone."

"But the people who probably shouldn't know she's gone already have her," Dennis pointed out.

"These cases are tricky," the man admitted. "Would you mind if I took your photo, miss? That would make the search much easier."

"Okay," Christine said. She'd never liked getting her picture taken. But if it would help…

The man reached underneath the counter and picked up an old-fashioned camera. The lens extended from the body on what looked like an accordion-folded sleeve. The lens itself was big and black. Several levers stuck up around it, making it look like the center of a mechanical flower.

The man lifted one edge of the counter and came out. Though his legs were covered in pants, he had no shoes over his goat's feet. Was he a satyr? He seemed too serious for that.

Christine stood in front of a blank wall as directed, while the man fiddled with the camera.

"Now, say *mead*," he instructed.

"Mead?" Christine asked. A bright flash blinded her.

Where had that come from? She hadn't seen a flashbulb on the camera.

"Perfect," the man said, looking at the back of the camera. "I'll put this on the watch list. See if someone comes in with a similar picture."

"Thank you," Christine said. She hesitated, then asked, "Since I just found out about, well, being a changeling. Uhm. Is there any way to find my birth parents?"

"Do you know if you were stolen? Or given up for adoption?" the man asked.

"Not a clue," Christine admitted.

"And there aren't going to be any baby pictures of you in your native form, correct?" the man asked.

Christine shook her head.

"I mean, you're welcome to look through the baby picture books. When kids get taken, they're usually reported. But I'm not sure it would do any good," the man told her.

"I see. Maybe some other day," Christine said.

It was just one more reason why she had to find Tina. Rescue her.

So that Christine could get some answers.

CHAPTER SEVEN

There wasn't anything Christine could think of doing before Friday and the wedding. The bachelor party had already happened, so they couldn't go crashing that. Dennis hadn't met the bride—Lars had claimed it was a girl he'd met in college.

Christine didn't want to break into Lars' family's house, particularly since she'd never been to their new house. Lars' family had moved once he'd graduated high school. Across the water, from Madison Valley to Mercer Island.

Had they only been in Madison Valley so that Lars could watch her? So that their families could be close?

Still, after Dennis had left for the evening, Christine felt restless. She'd spent a few hours curled up. Losing herself in a book. But now, she had to move again. Try something. Do something.

She snorted to herself. Maybe she *was* a troll of action.

With her charm and her illusionary self firmly in place, Christine walked out into the cold March mist. The night was gray, full of hazy rain. She didn't have a destination in mind. Just let her feet take her.

She found herself going north, up into Capitol Hill. Were there always this many people out at night? Hipsters, students, even older couples. The bars had people standing outside, smoking. More than one blasted loud music. Christine wasn't tempted to duck inside one, even when it started really raining.

Her feet kept moving her north. Up Broadway, past the construction and the light rail station, up farther. There were shops open, clothing stores and smoke shops and that funky place that sold everything.

For a moment, Christine was concerned that she was being compelled again. The DIY shop was farther up Broadway. Did she have to go back there?

But after another block, she found herself wanting to turn right. Then right again, going back the direction she'd come. She'd passed where she was supposed to go.

Finally, Christine stood in front of a P-Patch: a neighborhood garden where locals could apply for a small piece of land and grow what they liked. Flowers or vegetables or herbs.

A Japanese-style gateway led into the garden. It had a strange shimmer to it, as if it had been slicked down with oil.

There was *something* there. But what?

Christine hesitated. Should she call Dennis first? At least let him know where she was going? In case something happened?

That would be practical.

But Christine wasn't feeling practical that night.

Possibly for the first time in her life. Instead, she felt restless. Not compelled. Curious.

Heck with it.

Christine reached out and touched the gateway.

It jittered ever so slightly under her fingertips.

Interesting.

Here goes nothing.

Christine stepped through the gateway, expecting… something. Some kind of portal.

But everything was the same on one side as on the other.

That was a big nothing. Christine sighed, frustrated.

She should have just paid for a cab to get up to the Fremont troll. To find Patrick. She really wanted to talk with him some more.

Christine turned and walked back through the gateway.

But this time, winds gathered behind Christine, pushing at her. She turned her head as she took the next step.

When she looked forward again, she was someplace else. It took her a moment to realize that she now stood directly across from the Fremont troll.

How the heck had she done that?

No one noticed her stepping out from the shadows. The hubcap set in the eye of the troll glistened, sparkling *at* her.

Was that part of the portal? That she needed to be thinking of where she wanted to go? Would the arch in the International District do the same? Did she have to go from one special place to another? Or could she step directly from her home to somewhere else? Like the demons had? Like Ty had?

Christine eagerly looked for Patrick. He stood by himself, head bowed, next to the VW bus the troll grasped in one hand. He seemed to have pulled in on himself. Almost like he was shrunken. Smaller.

Christine walked over and stood beside him. After a few moments, Patrick finally raised his head. "Oh. Hello," he said. "You shouldn't be here."

"Why not?" Christine asked. Why was she so quick to anger now? She'd been happy to see Patrick, but now, she wanted to slap him.

"Anytime we gather here now, we get broken up," Patrick said. "It hasn't always been pretty."

"I'm sorry," Christine said. And she was. Was it all because of her? Because Lars was such an asshole? Or something else?

Christine glanced over her shoulder. Sure enough, two human-looking men, dressed in the same security uniform Lars had worn, were already making their way over.

"Do we have to gather here?" Christine asked. "Or could we go someplace else? And talk?"

"You know, I hadn't thought about that," Patrick said. "Except that, people expect me here. I always tell them to leave, though."

"You'll be back here tomorrow night," Christine pointed out. "And I really need some help."

Patrick nodded and looked thoughtful.

The two uniformed men came up close. Loomed.

Patrick caught Christine's eye. "Shall we?" he asked. Suddenly, Patrick stood up straighter. He came back into himself. He stood as tall as, if not taller than, either of the guards. He *loomed* right back at them.

Christine joined in after just a few moments. She would *not* be cowed by these two assholes.

The two guards seemed nonplussed.

Christine smirked. These guards weren't used to being challenged.

"We should get going," Patrick said after another moment, before it could escalate further.

Christine sighed, but nodded. It was probably for the best that they didn't get into a physical altercation.

Someday soon, she was going to learn how to physically fight. Because she wasn't always going to be willing to back down.

———

"Yes, we've always been here. Part of this earth," Patrick shouted over the sound of the crowd in the bar. At least there wasn't any music playing. They'd been lucky to find two seats together at a table in the corner. Crowds of young people, twenty-and-thirty-somethings, packed the rest of the place, overcrowding the tables, filling the seats at the bar, and standing in all the empty spaces in between.

Christine nodded and took another sip of her beer. The bar had been Patrick's suggestion. While there were quieter places they could have gone, no demon would hassle them here. It was too crowded, too public a place. Even on a Tuesday night.

Dennis would be shocked when she told him that she'd gone to a bar. Voluntarily. With a guy.

On a weeknight.

Patrick had been very happy to tell her of the history of the races. How there had always been hidden worlds. Yes, the humans wrote about them. But mostly got it wrong. They had their own history as well. Their own heroes and villains.

Christine could barely contain her excitement when he promised to bring her some books.

"What can you tell me about the portals?" Christine asked.

"Portals? What portals?" Patrick asked, puzzled.

When Christine explained how she'd gotten there, Patrick's eyes grew very wide. "Excuse me, but you're a troll, right?" he asked, after taking a large gulp of his beer.

"Yes," Christine said, nodding. "Green all over. With black hair. Tusks and fangs and claws." She found herself sitting up straighter when she described her true self, pride filling her voice.

She might have been shocked at the initial transition, but she did like it. In many ways, it felt more natural than her human self.

"Most trolls are not magical. They don't have the natural ability. And even if they do have power, they can't sense the world around them enough to be able to use it," Patrick said seriously.

"Is it because I'm a changeling?" Christine asked. "I was magically transformed for most of my life. Held in a different form with magic. So maybe I'm more used to it."

Patrick nodded. "That makes sense, now that you say

it. I'd be curious, though, what would happen if you were to train under a wizard for a while. If you could pick up spell casting."

Christine felt her eyes go wide. Her? Learn magic? Then she shrugged. "We'll see," she said. "I don't feel particularly magical."

"That's probably just a matter of training," Patrick pointed out.

"How does magic get inherited?" Christine asked. "If it turns out I'm magical, does that mean my parents were magical?"

"Chances are, if your parents had magic, you would. But not necessarily. You could have magic and they could have none," Patrick said. "I'm sorry. I know you'd like to find them."

"If they gave me up for adoption, would they have known I'd be used as a changeling?" Christine asked.

"No. No parent would give up their child knowing that was their fate," Patrick reassured her. "They loved you. They wanted a better life for you than they could have afforded."

A weight lifted off Christine's chest. That she'd been loved by someone who knew her true nature made her feel better than she'd anticipated. And that they wouldn't have voluntarily made her a changeling also eased her mind.

"You know...Never mind. I need to check something," Patrick said.

"What?" Christine asked.

"I'm sorry. I'm not a troll. You need to find someone of your own kind to ask these things. I know about the races in general. But I'm certain that a troll could answer so many more of your questions," Patrick said.

Christine nodded. That made sense. Was she going to have to come up here every night in order to find herself another troll? Or locate that place, what was it called, Trollville?

"I'll also ask around," Patrick said. "See if I can find someone who can help." He paused and sighed. "While we occasionally see trolls, they don't often join the group."

"Why is that?" Christine asked. She couldn't imagine that any of them had a problem with Patrick, even if he was an orc.

"They aren't as…peace-loving as we advocate," Patrick said.

"Ah," Christine said. She'd been feeling a lot less… peaceful, herself. She understood. It was just her nature, even though she hadn't been raised that way.

"Do any demons ever join?" Christine asked.

"No," Patrick said. He looked disgusted.

"What?" Christine asked.

"We did have one join. Once. He was a spy." Patrick took another swig of his beer. "Demons have a mistrustful nature. They couldn't believe that we would peacefully gather. Not ever."

"They really aren't the ones who are supposed to guide us, are they?" Christine couldn't believe that, not at all.

Patrick shrugged. "According to some texts, we are called *the lesser races.*"

"Texts?" Christine asked.

"Yes," Patrick said with a smile. "I'll see if I can find you some in English. You don't read Orcish, do you?"

Christine shook her head. She couldn't even read Trollish, if that was what it was called.

"Anyway, the demons are supposed to be our spiritual guides and mentors," Patrick added.

"That's bullshit," Christine said. "Really. It is."

"I know, I know. Don't get me started on it. But since the humans won the last battle, they've been lording it over us. Rewriting history. So that it was *destiny* for them to be in charge."

"When was the last battle?" Christine asked.

"Ten thousand years ago. Give or take a few centuries," Patrick said. "Not a lot survived from that time."

Christine nodded, surprised. Everyone talked as if it had just happened in the last decade. But it had happened that long ago?

"Is another big battle due? Is that part of the Great War?" That was all she could figure out.

"There are prophecies," Patrick said slowly. "But, there have *always* been prophecies. You live through a few and you get much less excited about them."

"Can I ask? How old are you?" Christine asked.

"You can ask," Patrick said with a slow smile. That was all he said.

"Lars said that Tina, my human doppelganger, had a Destiny. That he was going to twist it. She claimed to be important for the Great War. Is that enough to get your interest?" Christine asked. She wasn't about to ask if that would get him excited. She didn't know him well enough for that. Never planned to get to know him that well, either.

Patrick took another drink of his beer and thought.

"Possibly," he said. "The demons think she's very important, right?"

"Yes," Christine said, nodding.

"And this Lars is getting married this Friday, you said?" Patrick asked, leaning back and stroking his beard again.

"He is," Christine said. "We assume that whatever they're doing will be part of that ceremony." Dennis had double-checked—he still had his invitation. Lars had said they were still invited. Plus, there were well over two hundred other guests. Chances were, they wouldn't be checking the guest list too closely if they just showed up. It was a black-tie affair, out on their property on Mercer Island. She still needed to get a new dress, as well as a new pair of shoes. Her outfit needed to be elegant and practical.

"She probably isn't being kept out on their home property," Patrick said after a moment. "That's too risky."

"I know," Christine said. Ty had mentioned that as well. "We need to rescue her," she added.

"I agree with that, actually," Patrick told her. "Not because I think she's some kind of important princess," he said with distaste. "The humans really are full of themselves. But because it's the right thing to do. And," he paused, leaned closer, looking from side to side, as if to make sure that no one else was listening. "I'm tired of these demons bothering my group. It's about time to get a little revenge."

"Exactly," Christine said, keeping a straight face and not giving him a smug grin.

Nature would always win out. And they both had a fighting nature.

Christine agreed to meet Patrick the following night. He was going to teach her how to fight. There was a gym that *kith and kin* used, where she could fight as a troll.

Patrick, very gentlemanly, walked Christine back to the troll. Most of the tourists had gone, as well as the uniformed human security. The night had gotten colder. Before, Christine might have felt chilled. Now, it just invigorated her.

"I came out here," Christine told Patrick, finding the spot opposite the troll where she'd emerged.

"Interesting," Patrick said. "Okay, to get back, you need to have a clear picture in your mind of where you want to go. It doesn't have to be another portal. Just someplace you know well." He looked at where Christine stood, then back at the troll. "Do you see some sort of strange light around here?"

Christine pointed to the troll. "Reflected off the hubcap, there."

"You need to step into that light, then," Patrick said, stepping back.

She looked at the ground. There wasn't a pool or circle of light for her to step into. But the light from the troll felt like a steady beam. Not warm. But solid. Like a steady wind.

Christine imagined the corner by her apartment. The brick of her building, coming almost to the sidewalk. The tiny strip of dirt that held a round bush with yellow and green variegated leaves. The tiny crocus that were just starting to fade. The gentle swish of traffic.

With a single, breathless, step, Christine found herself standing on her corner. She almost fell over in shock. She hadn't expected it to work.

Did this mean she could get anywhere? If she'd been there before, and knew it well enough to imagine it? That's what Patrick had hinted at. Could she go someplace if she'd just seen a picture?

Google Maps might suddenly become her best friend.

Christine felt like she was floating all the way down the apartment building stairs to her place. She was going to learn how to fight. There might be a way of tracking her bio-parents. They were going to stop Lars and maybe ruin his wedding—always a bonus.

The claw marks on the outside of her door stopped her cold. What the hell?

The door was no longer locked. Christine pushed it open with her foot.

Someone had trashed her apartment. Ripped apart her papers. Standing in the vestibule, she could see the snowstorm that someone—some*thing*—had created from her books.

Christine felt sick to her stomach. She found her hands shaking. She shook them, trying to get them to stop. No luck.

Had they waited until she was gone before they attacked? Or had she just been lucky and missed them?

Christine's hands were still shaking so badly she could barely dial 911. Then she called Dennis and left a message, then left a message with Hannah as well.

Christine kept making herself take deep breaths. First, so that she wouldn't vomit. She stood at the edge of her living room, barely able to recognize it.

But also, because if she didn't, she'd start panting, snorting, and getting more angry.

And then she'd *troll out*, as it were. She touched her charm, but it was still cool under her fingertips.

She couldn't afford to go and get the bastards who had done this. Not yet.

But soon.

"What do you mean, the papers were misfiled?" Christine growled at her coworker. She stopped suddenly, realizing where she was. "I'm sorry," she said, leaning back. She loosened her hands at her sides, as she'd automatically made them into claws.

No one in the office even looked up at her outburst. The rest of the librarians and archivists continued their work, doing research or reading or filing, as if nothing was wrong.

Even Eva, Christine's coworker, merely looked apologetic. Not afraid. "I'll refile them this afternoon," she promised Christine.

After Eva had gone, Christine wondered again at the lack of reaction by anyone to her growl.

Perhaps she'd let more of her true nature show at work than she'd realized.

THE GYM WHERE CHRISTINE MET PATRICK DIDN'T look like much. Just a door in the side of a building in Ballard that was fortunately on a bus line that went direct from downtown. The parking lot was full of older cars. The building itself was done in pseudo-Tudor style, the white stucco needing repair in some patches, though the brown timbering looked in good shape. Pink neon letters over the door merely said, GYM. There were no windows in the two story building. No address numbers painted on the side.

What looked like a human sat behind the reception desk on the left, in a well-lit office. The hallway to the right was narrow and dark. Patrick waited for her just inside the door.

"Glad you could make it!" he exclaimed eagerly. He was already in shorts and a stained T-shirt that proclaimed, "It isn't really a debacle until someone catches fire."

He threw a look Christine couldn't interpret at the receptionist. *I told you so?* Or *Back off?*

"If you could just sign the waiver, Miss," the receptionist said, pushing forward a clipboard with a release form on it, basically stating that if Christine got injured on the property she wouldn't sue.

Christine signed the waiver and handed it back.

The receptionist gave her a huge grin that didn't seem to belong on a human face. "Nice charm you got there," he said. "Took me a while to see through it."

Christine was dying to ask the receptionist if he was a dwarf. Nik had said they could see through most illusions. Maybe she could ask Patrick about it later.

As they stepped into the dark hallway beside the desk, the lights suddenly came on. Motion sensor?

Except that Christine could now see the hallway was actually two. One led to the left. She assumed that was for the strictly human.

The one to the right had a magical glow. That was the only way she could describe the light. That same, shimmery quality that portals had. Blue-tinted, too.

By the time they reached the actual gym room, Patrick had changed into his native form. Christine tried not to stare.

Patrick had the same tusks she did, though his lower jaw was more prominent. His forehead was similar too, with a bony ridge across it. His ears were larger than hers as well as more rounded, less pointed. The color of his eyes had remained the same—still a watery blue. But he now had slits, not humanlike pupils. He wasn't green like she was. He was a mottled gray-and-reddish-brown, like rust-stained concrete.

The biggest change was his physique. Instead of looking like a ball, round and fat, he now had solid muscle across his chest and arms. No waist. Just muscle.

Christine didn't find him good-looking, necessarily, though she really did like his chest and the muscles. Would she find someone of her own species more attractive? She'd never really been drawn to any human males. She got a sense of that possibility, now.

Maybe the tusks were kind of sexy.

"You can change there," Patrick said, pointing out the door to the women's locker room.

Christine hurried across the gym, just getting a vague

impression of weights (and lots of them) on the right, while what looked like a boxing ring was on the left. While there was a faint odor of sweat, there were also spicy smells she couldn't identify.

Did the other races smell differently when they sweated?

The locker room was pretty simple: two rows of wooden benches with ceiling tall lockers on either side, with two showers just beyond, and a wall full of sinks and mirrors.

Christine took off her charm first, setting it carefully on the bench beside her. As soon as she was changed into her gym clothes, she tucked it carefully into a pocket. She didn't want to lose it, for anyone to steal it. Luckily, the shorts she'd found at the back of her closet were the stretchy kind, fit her new form, and had pockets.

Patrick led her over to the weights, explaining how they were starting with a bench press. He showed her the proper form, corrected her balance, then started her off with weights.

And more weights.

Benching her own body weight proved to be a lot easier than Christine would have imagined. She was much, *much* stronger than she'd been before. She was surprised at how good the exercise felt.

After a few more sessions with the weights, Patrick brought Christine over to the ring. He climbed up easily and swung himself over the ropes.

Christine found herself rooted to the concrete floor of the gym, unwilling to just climb up. It scared her in a way that she hadn't been scared of, not for a while.

For some reason, climbing up into that ring meant more of a change to her, meant accepting herself as a troll, more than she already had.

Christine took a couple of deep breaths.

"We don't have to do this," Patrick said, climbing back out of the ring and standing beside her.

"Yes, yes, I do," Christine said after a moment.

This was who she was, now. Someone who could lift weights and like it. Who could climb into a boxing ring and learn how to fight.

Her old self—the one that had been magicked into believing she was human—would never had done any of these things.

The realization that she'd changed struck her again.

She didn't have to be that girl anymore. Didn't have to be scared. Could go and change herself. Be who she wanted to be.

After another deep breath, Christine nodded. Smiled at Patrick.

"Let's do this."

CHRISTINE CLIMBED INTO HER BATHTUB GINGERLY. The water underneath the bubbles was almost blue with Epsom salts. Calming lavender filled the moist air. She sank into the water, relaxing and feeling slightly better immediately.

However, anxiousness buzzed under her skin.

Patrick had been easy, gentle on Christine, after she'd climbed up and stepped into the ring. Hadn't thrown her too much. Had shown her how to fall without hurting herself. How to break a hold. Some grappling.

It had also felt good to channel her anger, her aggression, in that fashion. She was still cleaning up her apartment. Would be for some time. Having an outlet like the gym would make the process easier.

Christine had never been in her own body like this before. She'd never gone out of her way to exercise, though she did like to walk.

To learn how to move, how to hold herself, how to attack and defend…it meant being aware of her bones and muscles and skin in a way she'd never done before.

She kind of liked it. She could see why jocks and exercise freaks got so involved in their workouts. All of it had felt good to her.

It didn't hurt that she was now naturally stronger, and seemed to be good at many things she'd never tried before.

A pounding at the door brought her out of her reverie.

"Who is it?" Christine called out. She tried not to growl. Too much.

"It's me. Dennis," her brother called out.

"And your mother," came another voice.

Crap. Had Dennis told Mum about her break-in? He was the worst gossip. She was so going to kill him later.

"I'm taking a bath," Christine admitted. She grabbed a towel and quickly dried off her hand before grabbing her charm, on the floor beside her. "Hang on!"

Would the charm short out in water? Nik hadn't mentioned anything like that. Christine slipped it over her head.

"Dennis, why don't you just let yourself in?" Mum asked.

Christine could tell her Mum was trying to keep her voice down.

"Mom, her place was just broken into. I'm not going to freak her out more by just barging in," Dennis whispered back urgently. "Give her some space."

Okay. So maybe Christine wasn't going to have to kill him later. Or maybe she'd make it a quick death.

She pulled the plug on the water and took another few moments to spritz herself off—leaving the soapy bubbles on her skin would just make her itch all night.

It was bad enough that her mother was here.

Christine rushed from the bathroom to her bedroom. At least the illusion had finally come back, making her look human. She firmly closed the bedroom door and called out, "Dennis. You can come in now. I'll be out in a sec."

She hadn't bothered with the chain on her door. The demons had only scratched the outside of the door as a warning. They hadn't actually broken in that way. They'd probably just come through a portal.

And that thought really hadn't helped her sleep at all the previous night, that they could just come back at any time, surprise her.

She needed to go back to Nikolai's Trade Goods and Emporium and get some protection. Sooner, rather than later.

While Christine threw on jeans and a loose-fitting blouse, she heard the front door open and shut.

She also heard her mother's barely stifled gasp when she reached the living room.

Christine double-checked in the mirror to make sure her illusion was firmly in place before she stepped out of her bedroom, walking the long hallway into her living room.

Mum stood in the center of the room, fists on her hips, her lips pressed together into a tight line. Christine hadn't had a chance to catalogue all the books that had been destroyed. The demons had also slashed up her nice bookshelves, broken the boards and clawed the backs and sides. She was going to have to refinish them all.

They'd also *despoiled* her reading chair. She wasn't sure if what they'd left on it was urine, crap, or a combination that only demons produced. She'd already taken it outside and left it next to the dumpster back there: the smell had been overpowering.

At least half of Christine's books had been reduced to snowflakes. Including the covers of the hardbacks, which she knew had taken some effort.

As the cops said, it had been a crime of passion. She must have really pissed someone off.

The demons had spray-painted graffiti across the windows and the books they hadn't torn to pieces. Red and black paint.

The room looked like it belonged in a horror movie.

They hadn't touched much else. Destroyed some papers and books out on the desk in the vestibule. But they hadn't gotten to her bedroom. Maybe she'd chased them off when she'd arrived.

Or maybe they were saving that for later.

"Right," Mum said after a few moments. "Do the police have any idea who might have done this to you?"

Christine took a deep breath. It was really bad when her mother's English accent came on so strongly.

"No, not really," Christine said. The human police certainly didn't have a clue. The *other* police, who she'd called after Hannah had gotten in touch with her, had confirmed that it was the work of demons. Of course, they had no ideas which ones.

Ty was going to come by the following evening to see if he could help.

Hannah had said she'd take on Christine's case if Ty could get a read on who had done it.

"You're not staying here another night," Mum declared. "Now, pack up a kit, let's go."

"No, Mum," Christine said firmly. "This is my apartment. They're not chasing me away. I'm staying here. I stayed here last night." She hadn't slept well, and her dreams had been…bloody.

Christine was more afraid of what she'd do if the demons came back than of what they might try. Particularly if they showed up while she was there.

"It isn't safe here," Mum pointed out.

How was Christine going to explain that it wasn't safe anywhere? That the demons hadn't come through the front door?

"I don't think it's much safer at your house," Christine said slowly. "I'll be fine, Mom."

"Then why did I have to hear about this from your brother?" Mum asked.

"Because he's a busybody who's always sticking his

nose in places where it doesn't belong?" Christine suggested. She was aiming for an innocent tone. Knew she'd missed it by a couple miles.

"Christine," Mum said, scolding.

"It's true," Christine maintained, trying to not let her anger boil over. Again.

"Well, at least let me come by and help you clean up," Mum said.

"This weekend. Sure," Christine said. "We could meet for breakfast." She doubted they'd get much accomplished. Mum was a night owl, who didn't really function until after 2 PM and a lot of coffee.

"Brunch?" Mum offered in return. "At 10. And you can also tell me about the changes that you're going through."

Christine held herself absolutely still. Oh, he had not. She glared at Dennis. He at least had the decency to look ashamed, though he shook his head slightly as well.

So he hadn't told her about the troll thing. Just that she was going through some things.

She was *so* going to kill him later.

"Mum," Christine said, then stopped. Paused. Thought about it. "I'll let you know when I'm ready." Because she honestly still didn't have any idea what she would say. How she would admit that she wasn't really family anymore. Or human.

"You know it's perfectly fine if you're a lesbian or something," Mum said too casually. "Your father and I have discussed the possibility."

"Thanks, Mum," Christine said. She really wasn't sure how to reply to that.

It wasn't that she disliked men. She'd just never found one that she was really attracted to.

She might never. A human man, at any rate.

A troll, on the other hand…she found herself still thinking about Patrick. His tusks. His muscles. Maybe she would be attracted to someone who was her own species. The same color of skin. The same types of claws.

"I'm not a lesbian," Christine assured her mother.

"Then what is it?" Mum pressed.

"I'm not ready to talk about it now," Christine said firmly. Damn it! Dennis should have known better than to tell Mum anything. She'd be horribly nosy about it until Christine told her something.

"You're not transgendered, are you? Because that would be okay, too," Mum said. "There's not a man living inside you, is there?"

"No, Mum there's not," Christine said, shaking her head. Where had her mother even *heard* the term "transgendered"?

Though this was Seattle.

"Your great-uncle Philip. I always wondered if he led a double life," Mum said. "It wouldn't have done for him to come out. Not in that day and age."

"Thanks, Mum, for the support," Christine said. "But it isn't anything like that."

"Are you pregnant? You know we'd love a grandchild. We'd work with you to take care of it," Mum said.

"All right. That's enough," Christine said. She couldn't believe the audacity of her mother. "You've seen my place. You've seen that I'm okay. You can go now."

Christine heard the words coming out of her mouth.

It was too late to bite them back. She'd never said something like that to her parents before. Ever. Even Dennis looked shocked.

"There's no need to be rude," Mum said. She brushed past Christine and marched down the hallway to the vestibule. "I know when I'm not wanted."

God, her Mum was such a drama queen.

"Mum, I promise, I'll tell you when I'm ready," Christine said. She shot Dennis a look that promised a tremendous amount of pain before following her Mum down the hallway. Not that she would ever actually hurt him. She was so much stronger than he was now. She wouldn't even wrestle with him. She'd find some other way, though.

"That's just it, dear," Mum said, pausing and looking back at Christine. "You've never really been ready, have you?"

"What do you mean?" Christine asked.

"You worked hard enough at school," Mum admitted. "But then you just…stopped."

Christine nodded. "I know." And she did. She knew what Mum was talking about. She'd stopped pushing. Had fallen into her books. Her routine.

"I promise you that this is a big enough change that things will be different," Christine said.

"You met someone," Mum said.

"No Mom. I haven't met anyone. Not yet," Christine said.

Mum stood in the hallway blinking for a moment. "You've never said *yet* before. You've always given me the impression that you weren't even interested in some kind of relationship." Mum smiled and reached out for Christine's hands. "You're *ready*."

Christine found herself nodding. "I…I think you're right, Mum. I mean, I have some other things to do first." *Like thwarting Lars. Rescuing Tina. Maybe saving the world.* "But I may be ready." It might take her some time for her to really get to know herself, all the parts of her troll self. However, the possibility was finally there. That maybe she could have someone else in her life.

"Why didn't you just tell me that?" Mum said, turning on Dennis. "Really. That was all you needed to say."

"I'm sorry?" Dennis said, confused.

"Men," Mum said with an over-exaggerated sigh. "But they can also be delightful, at times."

"You be sure to tell Dad I said hi," Christine said, feeling as uncertain about Mum's turn around as Dennis looked.

Mum took a hesitant step forward.

Christine met her halfway, gave her a quick hug.

It wasn't as bad as it normally was. Maybe Christine didn't have to worry so much about hugging her family. Maybe it would become more natural to her.

After Dennis and Mum had left, Christine returned to her living room. The mess would take forever to clean up. And she was going to miss those books. It would take forever to replace them.

But as Mum had said, Christine was finally ready. To try. To live. To love.

CHAPTER EIGHT

"Want to go crash a bachelorette party?"

Those weren't the first words that Christine had anticipated Dennis would say to her after their mum's visit. She knew an apology would be too much to hope for. Still, something more solicitous. Asking how she was doing. Even offering to come and clean on the weekend.

"Not really," Christine said as frostily as she could manage. She'd just gotten home from another day at the archives. While she liked her job—and she loved her papers and the quiet of the archives—she was afraid it didn't suit her as well as it once did. She took too much relish out of charging late fees to people who borrowed papers and didn't return them on time. She found herself contemplating setting up a booth outside the doors and charging admission to the archives themselves.

"Besides," she added, "Ty will be here in a while. He's going to see if he can identify the demons who trashed my place." And she wanted to go back to Nikolai's later that night—something else she didn't want to tell Dennis about. Particularly since she was going to meet Patrick there. She didn't want him to jump to the wrong conclusion. Or to complain about doing things without him.

She'd been doing things without him for a long while.

"And then you're going to Nikolai's, right?" Dennis asked innocently.

"How did you know?" Christine asked, sagging onto her bed. She couldn't really go out and do much in the living room, not until Ty got there. She was afraid any trace might already be obliterated by all the people passing through. And the cleaning she'd already done.

It was such a huge task. Taking the heart out of her.

"Talked with Patrick," Dennis said, sounding smug. "So this bachelorette party? Is actually taking place *in* the International District. Near Nikolai's."

"Where," Christine said flatly. She wasn't agreeing to go on this wild goose chase. But she might as well know the worst of it.

"Some demon club," Dennis said breezily.

"What?" Christine growled. "What do you mean?" He wasn't actually suggesting that she go to some club that was run by demons, was he?

"It's this underground club. It's just for your kind. No humans or angels allowed," Dennis said. "Isn't that cool?"

Christine wasn't sure how she felt about her brother knowing more about *her* stuff than she did. "Cool" wasn't a word she'd use, however.

"Is it safe?" Christine asked. She knew what damage a demon could do. Just take a look at her living room.

Though that had been against her poor, defenseless books. Not her own tough hide.

"It should be. Especially if you go with Patrick. Maybe you could pretend to be dating, or something," Dennis suggested.

"No," Christine said firmly.

"But—"

"Absolutely, one hundred percent, no," Christine said, shuddering. "He's an *orc*."

"And?" Dennis asked.

Christine shook her head, though she knew Dennis couldn't see her. "I find him as attractive as you find Lucy, your dog."

"Oh," Dennis said, sounding defeated. "It's like that? Between the various races?"

"Yeah, it's like that." Christine heard the sigh coming from the other phone. "Look, it's why Mum thought I might be a lesbian. Because I'm not attracted to human men at all. And no, you have *not* heard the last of that yet."

"Huh?" Dennis asked. "I don't follow you."

"Men? Human men? Not attractive to me," Christine said. "Also—orcs. And some of the other species I've seen. However. If I could find a troll someday—"

"Ah ha!" Dennis said. "We just have to set up a profile for you on a dating site for your kind. You have dating sites, right?"

"I haven't a clue," Christine growled. "And I don't care right now."

A knock on the front door saved her.

"I'll call you tomorrow to coordinate, before the

wedding," Christine told Dennis. "But I don't want to hear from you before then."

"You know I just have your best interests at heart, right?" Dennis asked.

"That kind of thing may have been charming when you were a teenager. You're not anymore," Christine told him. He didn't have to push at her so much anymore. She was perfectly capable of moving forward on her own, now. She hadn't spent a quiet night, just sitting and reading, in what felt like ages.

She *was* a troll of action, after all.

"I'll talk with you tomorrow." She stabbed the phone off, then immediately set it to mute so she wouldn't hear it if Dennis tried to call her back.

She'd just been rude. She knew it. But she wasn't his passive sister to be wheedled into doing things his way.

She loved her brother. Her family. She still didn't know how they'd react to her true form. Whether even Dennis was going to be able to accept the changes she was going through, not so much in looks, but in personality.

She didn't want to lose them.

She wasn't sure she had a choice. If they weren't already gone. Broken like the spell that had once kept her human-looking.

"I'M SORRY," TY SAID. HIS VOICE SOUNDED HIGHER and clearer in his half-human, half-hound form. He wore a blue jumpsuit over his regular clothes, he'd explained to contain contamination. "But the demons were clever this time."

"How so?" Christine asked, trying to swallow her disappointment. She'd really wanted to find some trace of them. Hannah had called her back once already, asking for news. She'd even promised to do the case for free if she thought they could win.

"The demons—at least half a dozen of them—came from four different planes. Maybe more." Ty sighed, frustrated. "There are too many traces. I can't tease them all apart."

"Thank you anyway," Christine said.

Ty looked out at her wrecked living room and shook his head. "Damn shame." Then he turned and started packing away his equipment.

"I appreciate the effort," Christine told him honestly. She still felt disheartened. So many of her books had been ruined. It was going to take so long to replace them, if she ever could.

"It's just frustrating, you know?" Ty said. "They come over here all the time. Break the DHIVRT treaty with impunity. But they never seem to get caught at it."

"Are the courts crooked?" Christine asked. Judges, lawyers, even juries got bought sometimes.

Ty shrugged. "They don't make it that far in the system. It's like—the whole system is designed to hide them. Protect them. Or something."

For some reason, that brought Lars' boast of twisting Tina's fate, her Destiny, for their use. "Could they have done something like that?" Christine paused. "I mean, they've been preparing for this Great War of theirs for a while, right? Could they have also prepared some kind of protection? Something that, I don't know, warped reality around them, so they were never caught or seen?"

Ty paused, thinking. "That implies a heavy-duty amount of organization," he said slowly.

"They moved to my neighborhood just so one of them could become friends with my brother and watch my family," Christine pointed out. "That seems to me to imply a fantastic level of planning."

Ty nodded, then he looked back around the living room. "I'd like to come back later, if I could. I want to test for something else. That kind of protection or cloaking. I've never thought to check for it before. I've just always thought they were lucky."

"I'm going out for a while…" Christine said.

"Sure, sure, no problem. Tomorrow morning? Before work?" Ty asked. "It's important."

"Okay," Christine said. She really wanted to nail these assholes.

She just needed to find something that would stick.

BECAUSE TY SEEMED TO BE ABLE TO TRACK PEOPLE based on where they entered a portal, Christine walked to P-Patch community garden before accessing a portal. Patrick had told Christine that with training, she could set up her own portal anywhere, like Ty did.

Hopefully, though, whatever portal she set up wouldn't be as messy as Ty's.

The night had grown cold, cold enough that

Christine watched her step. Would the sidewalk freeze? It had been misty-raining all day. There was just enough moisture in the air that it was freezing cold. Even with her thicker skin, it still seeped into Christine's bones. She was looking forward to being inside again. And soon.

Of course, there were students on the sidewalk. But also shoppers. Music pounding out whenever a door to a bar opened. Street kids with guitars, playing for tips. Even a guy with a table set up, giving tarot card readings. She might have to come back and see if he was really magic or not.

Christine hadn't realized that she lived in such an active place. She liked her apartment because it was close to her work.

Maybe Dennis was right. She *should* get out more.

Not go to bars or listen to music. That was still too loud. But there were a lot of nice coffee shops. She could go to one of those, curl up with a good book, and read.

No one would bother her.

And if they did, she wasn't as scared as she'd once been. She had a better idea of who she was. And she was strong.

A long, low whistle brought Christine's thoughts back to the sidewalk. A drunken homeless man with long greasy hair and a scraggly beard stood a few feet in front of her. He wore army fatigues, the jacket not buttoned up correctly, jeans with cuffs caked in mud, and bare feet.

"That's some mighty fine sugar you got there," the man cackled.

His friends, already camped out along the edge of the

sidewalk, curled up in the doorway of the abandoned restaurant, were trying to pull the drunkard back.

"You gonna share it with me?" The homeless guy cracked up at his own joke.

"No," Christine told him. She made herself look him directly in the eye. "Leave me alone."

"Hoo hoo! All high and mighty," the drunk sneered.

Christine stepped around him and kept going. Her heart raced in her chest. Her mouth grew dry. She normally would have just rushed by, not looked at him, not engaged.

She really was getting brave. Or stupid.

"You'll regret it later!" the drunk called after her. "End days is coming!"

Christine didn't stop. He was just some crazy guy. She did glance over her shoulder.

His eyes held a red gleam.

Christine shuddered as she turned back, hurrying down the sidewalk.

Was he some kind of demon? Why would he get drunk that way, if he had that kind of power? Or was he possessed? Did demons possess people?

Christine made her way as quickly as possible to the P-Patch. Maybe Patrick could tell her.

The arch glowed with the same slick light she'd seen before. The night seemed to have grown even colder. Plants in the garden glistened from the rain, as if anticipating the coming frost. The air smelled wet and earthy.

Christine had to wait while a couple made their way

up the street, holding hands and leaning close to one another.

She'd never been too lonely. Maybe now, though, she didn't have to be at all.

With the gateway to Chinatown firmly in her mind, plus added pictures from the internet, Christine stepped through the arch to the P-Patch.

Nothing happened. Not even a glimmer.

She tried it again.

Still no luck.

She thought about the troll and inched toward the gateway. Her skin tingled. If she continued forward, she could go to the troll. Not a problem. She tried the same thought experiment, considering her apartment. Again, the portal worked without a problem.

She just couldn't go to the gateway in the International district.

What the hell?

What was close to there? Could she step into Nikolai's shop?

Almost. It felt like the gate was stuck. There was a barrier there that she just couldn't push through. It wasn't just the Chinese gate, but a huge circle around it.

Christine thought about the large pillars that held up the freeway, on the edge of the International District. They'd been painted red, with gold koi circling them.

One step later, she was standing next to them.

Why couldn't she get closer? Why was that gate blocked? And was it just blocked to her? To trolls? Or to all peoples?

Christine could walk into the International District without a problem. But she couldn't arrive magically.

Just one more thing to ask Patrick about. One more thing to learn about.

She'd spent a lifetime learning human culture. She wished she had another to learn all about her native culture, now.

It hadn't taken anytime at all for Christine to find the entrance to Nikolai's shop. She could see it now, the dark blue around the human door. It worked like the other portals—step up with a firm idea of where she wanted to go, then step through.

Were there other shops that this portal connected to? How did she discover them?

The wooden shopkeeper already had customers when Christine walked in. He still looked up, his painted mouth smiling at her. "Shopping for something particular?" he called.

"Protection charms," Christine told him.

"Aisle four," Nikolai instructed before turning back to his existing customers.

Christine wandered over to the fourth aisle. She immediately found the *ba guas* that Ty had recommended, bright yellow and orange, with different length lines around the eight sections surrounding the mirror in the middle. She chose three that were about the size of her troll palm. One to hang in the hallway leading to her apartment, another to put above the shelves in her living room. The third was for Dennis. They were cheap enough, and it wouldn't hurt for him to have some protection as well.

The kits fascinated her. They were in English and contained all the ingredients for making a protection charm herself. The box showed a cartoon demon being repelled all the way across a room after merely looking at a charm.

The same charm, already assembled, was three times as expensive.

Nikolai nodded with approval when she came up to the counter. "These are good," he said, indicating the kit. "You should come and show me your results, when you finish."

"I will," Christine said. Because the kit was also very clear that it took no responsibility for ill-made charms.

"Protecting your home?" Nikolai asked slyly.

"Yes," Christine admitted. "We're not really tourists," she said softly.

"Changeling?" Nikolai guessed.

Christine gave a great sigh of exasperation. Something needed to be done about the humans stealing troll babies.

"It's okay," Nikolai said softly. "As a shopkeeper, I keep many secrets. And I will help, if I can."

Christine knew he wasn't lying.

She also knew that if she managed to screw up making the charm completely, he'd be happy to sell her more protection.

"So why couldn't I come directly here?" Christine asked as she sipped the bubble tea Patrick had insisted she try. It was too sweet, yet at the same time, strangely addictive. She couldn't stop drinking it until she was finished with it.

They walked up the hill from the light rail station, heading toward the bar that held the bachelorette party.

"I don't know," Patrick said. "Maybe it's something to do with your race. The gate's open."

"Hmmm," Christine said. She knew there was something more. "Is the International District, well, controlled by demons?"

Patrick shook his head. "No more so than Pioneer Square is. Or Bellevue. There's a mix everywhere." He paused, then added, "In some places, the mix is more demon-heavy. Or angel heavy. It just depends. And maybe the ID is more demon than angel."

"Could it be because of the party tonight?" Christine asked. "That they'd asked to have the gate closed for one night?"

"That doesn't make sense, since the bar isn't on top of the gate, but farther up the street. And you said you could get into the district walking," Patrick pointed out.

Christine sighed, frustrated. There had to be an explanation. And it had to be the demons behind it.

"So what should I be expecting tonight?" Christine asked after a few more steps.

"It will be loud," Patrick warned. "Probably really dissonant." He shuddered.

It was going to be as bad as—if not worse than—the other night. (Was it less than a week ago?) With all the loud music and snotty kids and feeling as though she didn't belong.

At least this time she didn't have to pretend she was there to have fun.

THE BOUNCER SAT BEHIND A GLASS BOOTH, JUST inside the door. He barely looked at them. He wasn't human. Christine was certain of it. But then again, neither were they. He took their money and waved them in.

Of course, the club was underground. For the first time, it didn't make Christine feel better to be going downstairs.

There was more than one bar in the club. Christine and Patrick found the bachelorette party in the Silk Lounge, on the lowest level.

The room was long and narrow. Black polished marble made up the walls, with tiny white veins squeezed into the rock. A black, sleek bar took up one side. Modern. Spare. With discreet lights highlighting the liquor and the shelves beyond it. Tiny flickering bulbs set into the bar itself gave it an eerie glow.

Patrick and Christine sat at the back, as far away from the band as they could get. Light imitating flames leapt up the walls opposite the bar. The tables—tiny, round metal tops balanced on black metal legs—were mostly full. The chairs were surprisingly comfortable leather, with rounded backs. On wheels, so Christine and Patrick could easily pull closer, then wheel apart.

A postage-stamp-sized dance floor lay in front of the

band. No one danced. Huge speakers, taller than Christine, and wider than her and Patrick combined, stood in all four corners of the dance floor.

There might be enough volume to make Christine's ears bleed if she stood in the center of them.

There were at least three guitarists, a drummer, and a one-armed keyboardist. He fascinated Christine, as he seemed to have the most energy of all the band members, attacking the keys with one hand. Then swinging his head to whip his long hair out of the way. He was also bearded, dressed in leathers, heavyset. Looked like an aging '70s rocker.

The bachelorette party had half a dozen of the tiny tables pulled together, teetering with drinks. The party itself was loud. Christine could hear their shouting over the screeching of the band. At least eighteen women were gathered there. Many of them were very drunk, leaning on each other and giggling hysterically. Or swaying to the music in their chairs. Completely un-self-conscious, the way only drunk people could be.

The bride-to-be was easily identified by the large black-and-red sash draped from shoulder to hip that announced her as "Doomed." She had a plastic ball-and-chain shackle around one ankle. She was pretty enough, in a Botticelli sort of way, with a high Roman nose and dark features. She wore her black hair piled high on her head, with a sparkling tiara.

"So what do we do now?" Christine asked Patrick (by yelling in his ear) after they'd ordered their drinks and watched the bachelorette party screech at each other. And laugh. A lot.

"I'm not sure," Patrick admitted. "Do you know any of the girls?"

Christine looked over at the table again. They were mostly about her age. But they were like Lars and his friends. At least half a dozen, maybe more, steps up the social ladder. They wore designer shoes and dresses. Their hair was professionally cut and dyed. They'd spent more at the eyebrow bar at Macy's than Christine had spent on rent.

"No," Christine said. "I wouldn't." She hadn't ever even wanted to be like these women. The only part she envied was the ease in which they seemed to navigate life. The confidence they exuded.

The band continued to prance wildly around the stage, trying to generate some interest in their music. The dance floor stayed empty. Only the bachelorette party seemed to be having fun. The couples at the other tables drank silently and heavily.

Just as Christine was about to suggest that they leave, Patrick leaned over to her and said, "Now! Go! Now!"

"What?" Christine asked.

Then she saw what he'd seen. The bride-to-be was leaving the table, telling her friends to stay behind. Heading to the restrooms. Alone.

"Go too!" Patrick told Christine.

Christine rolled her eyes, but did as Patrick suggested. What was she going to say to the woman, though? It wasn't as if she could just go up and introduce herself. Or announce that Lars was a demon. Chances were, the bride was a demon herself.

The bathroom didn't have an attendant sitting outside

of it, which surprised Christine. She'd figured someplace this fancy would.

However, the front sitting lounge was as big as her living room. When she closed the door behind her, the noise from the bar disappeared. Christine breathed a huge sigh of relief.

No wonder the bathroom was so big. Women could come back here to escape the noise. It also explained why there wasn't an attendant. Someone in charge understood that it was better to let the women have their moment of peace, alone. No one there to watch them.

The other woman wasn't there in the lounge, though. Christine heard noise from one of the stalls past the lounge. All the stalls were in separate compartments with wooden doors carved with scrolls and columns. They looked like priestly confessionals. The toilets themselves were black (of course) and each compartment had its own sink, scented soap, and soft towels.

Christine went into the one closest to the bride-to-be's. Then she sat there, waiting. She actually didn't want to leave. It was peaceful and quiet.

Maybe she should spend a night just curled up, reading, and not doing anything else.

After five minutes had passed, Christine made herself open the door to her stall.

The other girl sat in the large lounge, all by herself, her back turned toward the door.

Was she crying?

Christine didn't want to interfere. It wasn't…polite.

Still. The girl *was* crying. And they did need information.

"Excuse me," Christine said softly, holding out one of the soft towels to the girl.

"Oh, oh, no, I'm fine," the girl said automatically. She looked at the towel Christine was holding out. "Thanks," she said, taking it, wiping her eyes.

"Aren't you, aren't you the bride? I mean, to be?" Christine asked, stumbling over her words.

The girl teared up again. "Yes! Yes, I am," she said. Then she turned her head and started crying in earnest. "No, I'm not," she admitted quietly.

"What happened?" Christine said, sitting down next to her.

The girl grabbed Christine's hand. It was hot and her fingers felt like bones against Christine's skin. "He *dumped* me. For this girl he didn't even know existed!"

"That's awful!" Christine sympathized, trying to twist her arm a little, get the girl to loosen her grip.

"But I still have to pretend!" the girl whined between her tears. "That's the worst part. Everyone has to think I'm still the bride!"

"Why would he make you do that?" Christine asked. Who was Lars marrying if he wasn't marrying this girl? And why the circus?

"I *have* to go through with it. My family would *kill* me if I didn't. There's some stupid prophecy that the two ceremonies will fulfill," the girl said. Then she put her hand in front of her mouth and looked at Christine with horror. "I wasn't supposed to say that."

"Say what?" Christine asked, trying to put the girl at ease. "I didn't understand it anyway," she added.

Though she did. Her mind raced to put the pieces together.

This girl was the original bride. Who Lars had originally intended on marrying. Some sort of demon, no doubt. Particularly given the way her hand clawed at Christine.

But now that Tina had shown up, Lars had dumped this girl. Or rather, was only going to play at being the groom for her. Make her go through with the wedding, or at least, the ceremony. Possibly leaving her at the altar.

It wasn't just that he was going to twist Tina's destiny. No, it was much worse.

He was going to marry her.

THERE WASN'T ANYTHING THEY COULD DO ABOUT THE wedding until the next day, Friday, the actual day of the affair. Even then, they didn't have much of a plan beyond, "Show up, rescue Tina, ruin the blood ceremony."

No one could tell Christine what the blood ceremony would entail. She assumed Tina would end up dead. And maybe other people as well.

Dennis was insistent that he could only bring Christine to the wedding, that she couldn't also bring Patrick. "It says *plus one*, and Lars' family are kind of sticklers for that kind of thing," he told her over the phone.

"We're already kind of crashing the wedding," Christine pointed out.

"Lars said I was still invited," Dennis said stubbornly.

"What if just Patrick and I went?" Christine asked. She stood in her kitchen, pondering the ingredients for the charm laid out on the counter. Salt she understood. Even iron flakes. But oregano? Fresh sage and rosemary? And powdered, dried cumin?

The charm was supposed to repel demons. Not make them hungry.

"No, I need to go," Dennis said stubbornly. "I want to see this through. Lars was *my* friend."

"He *pretended* to be your friend," Christine pointed out. "So you may not be welcome."

"Neither may you," Dennis reminded her. "But…I just…I want to see this through."

"I don't want you to get hurt," Christine told her brother. She would kill any demon who tried.

"I don't want you to get hurt either," Dennis said. "So we both should go. Watch each other's back."

Christine finally relented. "All right," she said with a sigh. "But if they kill you, I'm so not taking the blame." Though she knew her mother would never forgive her if she let her baby brother get killed.

Dennis gave a snorting laugh. "If they kill you, I'm sure there will be hell to pay."

After Dennis had hung up, Christine found herself still caught on that phrase.

Would they make Hell pay? Christine wasn't sure. Or was Hell paying already, and was everyone dancing to their tune?

It was all part of a larger picture. She was certain of it.

But for now, Christine had a charm to assemble. She'd never been a good cook. But she had all the ingredients. It would just be a matter of putting them together, right?

Christine carefully measured out the iron flakes and the oregano, placing them in the glass mixing bowl. She chopped up the rosemary as fine as she could get it. She needed to either sharpen her knives or buy new ones. Or this rosemary was particularly tough.

The iron pot had been tricky, but she'd found one at the local second-hand store. It smelled like rancid bacon. Even after she'd cleaned it. Hopefully that wouldn't make a difference.

The dough part turned out to be trickier than Christine had imagined. Her flour would get dough-like, then turn rock solid, in two seconds time after she added the powdered, blessed crystal. She literally timed it. Why was it setting so hard? So quickly?

Luckily, Christine had enough of both the flour and the crystal powder to try it a third time. She added more water. The crystals remained the same. As soon as she stuck a spoon into the mixture and started stirring, the crystals sucked in all the water and hardened.

But this time, Christine was ready. She had the rest of the ingredients close at hand, and she poured them in before the mixture set again.

She'd have to be sure to ask Nikolai what that meant. Why she couldn't take her time creating a charm. Why it completed almost before she was finished.

Did it have magic? She held it up to the light and looked at it critically. She'd tried forming the dough into a braid during the two seconds it had been pliable. However, it just looked like a misshapen lump. Bulbous at one end, then narrowing down. Not like one of those Swedish breads. Not like the picture at all.

There wasn't any way for her to test if it was magic. Was there? She couldn't see magic. Though she had seen the magic at the Chinese gateway, as well as the P-Patch.

Though Nikolai had said it didn't matter, Christine took off her charm. Then she turned off the lights. She saw almost perfectly well in the dark, now. Though she'd checked a couple of times, her pupils just got big and round, and didn't elongate like a cat's.

The charm didn't glow. She sprinkled water on it. It didn't suddenly take on that slick appearance either, like the gates had.

Had the magic worked? She wasn't sure. It didn't feel that way. It still just looked like an oddly shaped hunk of dough.

She was going to have to pay triple the price to have something effective in her apartment, wasn't she?

Still. She felt oddly proud of it. Despite how ugly it looked.

Christine took one of the kitchen chairs, taped a piece of red string to the back of the charm, and hung it over the doorway to her living room.

Take that. Christine giggled. As if any demons would heed her.

CHAPTER NINE

CHRISTINE WIGGLED HER TOES IN HER NEW SHOES. They were two sizes bigger than she used to wear. They also had a large enough toe box to be comfortable. At least they looked pretty, made of black leather, with kitten heels and a rounded toe. Strap over her ankle. Practical. She could run in them if necessary.

And they matched her new dress. (Again, she was spending far too much money!) It wasn't like she would wear this kind of outfit often, navy blue and formal. However, she secretly *loved* it, the way the hem cut asymmetrically from one side to the other, the fullness of the skirt, how it cinched in around her waist. It was sleeveless, cut high around her neck but open in the back.

It was the kind of dress she'd always wanted to wear. Had never had the courage to.

Dennis drove the pair of them to the wedding. The event was taking place on Lars' family's estate on Mercer Island. She assumed the richer part of the island. The house hadn't shown up on the GPS, which did but didn't surprise Christine. At least it was here, close to Seattle. Christine could possibly have gotten a bus there, at least to the island. At least it wasn't in the boonies like Lars' family vacation home in the San Juan Islands.

The road had turned, then divided off the main street. Become narrow and twisty. No place to pull off. Rocks and forest growing close to the edge of the pavement. Then the wind picked up. And the rain. Lights were few and far between.

They passed from one end of the road to the other, without seeing a turn-off.

Grudgingly, Dennis handed Christine the tiny map that had been included in the invitation. "See if you can spot the driveway."

"Haven't you been here before?" Christine asked as Dennis turned the car around.

Dennis shrugged. "Once or twice. But not in the last year."

They started back down the twisty street. "You sure you don't need the light on or something?" Dennis asked.

"I'm sure," Christine told him. Though being in a car gave her slight vertigo now, making her carsick, having the map to read actually helped. Lights wouldn't have.

"Turn here," Christine directed Dennis after less than half a mile.

Dennis slammed on his brakes then took the turn hard. "I swear that driveway wasn't there the first time we drove by it," he muttered.

The "driveway" was just a track cut into the trees. Grass grew in between the tire tracks. Branches reached out and brushed the sides of the car. The headlights flashed on patches of colored flowers as the road curved. The car wheels skipped and churned as the path grew steep.

"Are you sure…" Dennis' question faded as they reached the top of the hill.

Suddenly, they were on pavement. An elegant drive curved off to the right, then circled back. A huge brick-and-stone mansion, at least three stories high, dominated the space. Fountains and flowers graced the center of the wide driveway. White lights flooded the area, making it seem like they were in the middle of downtown.

Tall white men in formal tuxes and tails, wearing white gloves, rushed over to open the car doors. "Greetings," said one, holding out his hand for Christine to take. "Welcome!"

Of course, it wasn't really raining here. Only on the road. Where mere mortals trod.

"Thank you," Christine said, putting her hand on top of his and stepping out of the car. She should have figured that Lars and his family would have liveried servants. She waited to the side while Dennis handed over the keys to his car. Of course, the servants were too well trained to sneer at his Toyota Camry. Maybe Dennis was just *choosing* to slum it tonight. Didn't want to show up the groom by arriving in a fancier vehicle.

"Friend of the bride? Or friend of the groom?" asked a much older gentleman. He was also formally dressed, and held a small electronic tablet in one gloved hand. He looked like the stereotypical butler that Christine had read about, with a bald head but fringes of white hair still around the edges, a superior nose matched with a superior attitude.

"Both, actually," Christine said, stepping forward. "My brother went to school with Lars, while I've known the bride forever."

"Very good," the butler said. He peered critically at Dennis. "Yes. I thought I recognized you. The Tuckermans, correct?"

"Yes," Dennis said. He stood stiffly next to Christine.

Would they still be on the list? Invited into the house? Had Lars uninvited them at the last minute? Christine was surprised that they were checking the guests so carefully.

Then again, if it really was this important of an event, maybe they would.

"Welcome," the butler said after verifying their names on his device. "There are actually two celebrations going on. One in the front room, for friends of the groom," he said, nodding his head toward Dennis. "And a second, upstairs, for the bride."

Was it better for them to split apart? Christine couldn't protect Dennis that way. In movies, that was always the most stupid thing to do.

"I'll be fine," Dennis assured Christine.

God, she hated this. She just wanted to growl and pull him close. This felt like she was sending him into danger.

But they weren't going into an actual battle. Yet.

Before Christine could say anything, another liveried servant appeared. "This way," he said, directing Dennis inside.

She had her cell phone. Dennis could always call if he

was in trouble. She nearly snorted. Like he'd call for help. He wouldn't even stop to ask for directions.

Still. She had to trust that he'd be okay. That she'd be able to find him later.

And tear to pieces anyone who had hurt him.

"MIGHT I SAY, MISS, THAT YOU DO LOOK FAMILIAR," the butler confided as he walked Christine down a long hallway. Dozens of framed photos covered the sage-colored walls. Lars when he was a child. The family standing in front of a crystal blue lake. Older relatives in less modern clothes. Lars' mother as a child and a young woman. Lars' father in his military uniform.

Shit. Did the butler know Tina? Had he seen her? Christine had been worried about that from the start. "I don't think so," she said evasively.

"I never forget a face, ma'am," the butler said loftily.

"Maybe I just look like someone else you know," Christine found herself saying. Then she pressed her lips together. She shouldn't have said that either.

"Possibly," the butler said. He hesitated in front of a closed door. Looked at her. Hard.

"Then it will come to you later," Christine said, resigned. This operation had never been a guaranteed success.

"It will," the butler promised. He opened a wooden paneled door beside them. "This way, ma'am."

Christine stepped through the door. The room beyond was decorated especially for the wedding. White tulle was draped between the windows as well as hanging from the center chandelier to the walls. Sparkling streamers, proclaiming, "Happy Days!" ran across the walls. The walls were an orangeish-beige color, matching the dark wood chairs that circled it.

In the far corner, a woman sat on a couch in the middle of a sea of white—her fairy-princess bride dress. It was the same woman Christine had met at the bar. Half a dozen other women sat around her, holding her hand while she cried.

Christine took a step toward the group, then paused. Something tugged at her. Something vaguely familiar.

She turned. To the left stood another paneled door, painted dark red-brown, firmly shut.

None of the other group had looked up and seen Christine yet. She quickly walked over to the other door.

It was unlocked.

Christine slipped inside. Gasped.

There, on the tiny single bed shoved into the corner, sat Tina. She wore a plain shift, made out of unbleached muslin (all the better to sacrifice you in, my dear!).

Tina looked blankly at Christine. "Hello," she said softly. "Who are you?"

<hr>

"Tina," Christine said urgently, walking toward the bed. "I'm your friend. I'm here to get you out of here." The room held a tall wooden dresser on one side. A tiny table stood next to the iron-framed bed. Near the end of the bed, a window looked out into the night.

Tina wrinkled her brow, looking puzzled. "Why do I need to get out of here? I'm getting married," she confided in Christine.

Was it too late? Had Lars already *twisted* Tina?

Christine looked around the room. There was only the one door in and out of the room. There was the window, but they were up on the third floor. Christine wasn't sure she could make it without breaking a leg, regardless of how strong she'd grown.

At the foot of the bed, leaning against the wall with the door, stood another antique chest, dark and heavy. While Christine could use it to barricade them both in the room, what good would that do them?

Christine cautiously approached the bed, watching Tina carefully. But she didn't pull back, just smiled at her. She perched on the edge of the bed and took one of Tina's hands in her own. It felt cold and small. No shock this time. No sudden recognition or shakeup of the world.

"Don't you remember me?" Christine said. "You're my sister. My twin. Remember?"

Tina searched Christine's face with wide eyes, then burst out laughing. "Silly. We don't look anything alike."

What did Tina see? Did she see Christine's troll body? Or just her darker human self?

"We're practically identical," Christine assured her. "We only met a week ago. For the first time. In that bar on Madison. Remember?"

"I've always wanted to have a sister," Tina said wistfully. She sighed and shook her head. "It's too late now."

"No. It isn't. Tina. Christine. I know you're in there somewhere. You've got to fight this!" Christine told her.

"I don't know what you're talking about," Tina complained. "Fight what?"

"You're important," Christine told her. "You have a Destiny."

"I *know* that," Tina said giggling. "It's to marry Lars. To bring peace to both our peoples."

Twist her destiny. "No. He's trying to win the Great War," Christine insisted.

"I know that's what you've been told," Tina said confidentially. "But it isn't true. Lars is truly a wonderful man. A savior."

Christine opened her mouth, then shut it again. Telling Tina her opinion of Lars wouldn't help matters any.

She looked around the room again. There wasn't anything there. Nothing magic. No portal. No way of getting out of the room other than through the door. And Tina wouldn't go with Christine. She'd been brainwashed. Enspelled.

"Here," Christine said. She took Tina's hand and tried to wrap it around her own illusion charm. That had magic in it. Maybe that would prompt something in Tina.

"It's pretty?" Tina said, pulling back. "But I'm not sure what you want."

"I want you to come with me," Christine admitted.

"I think I should probably call for the butler, now," Tina said, pulling back further. "He has magic. He'll take care of you."

"You should rely on your own magic," Christine

pointed out to her. "Not someone else's."

"Silly," Tina said. "I don't have any magic left. It's all gone, now," she added sadly.

Was all her magic gone? Or had Lars tricked Tina into thinking she was powerless?

"Look, if I prove to you that I'm your sister, your twin, will you at least listen to me?" Christine asked.

Tina looked uncertain, then nodded, slowly.

How could she do this? They hadn't actually been raised together. But their human selves were almost identical. Tina had said they'd been bonded magically since they were babies. Maybe their physical tastes were the same as well.

"You prefer savory to sweet," Christine started with. "You'd rather have garlic cheese bread over chocolate cake, any day."

"How did you know that?" Tina asked, surprised.

"Because I know you," Christine said. "You don't really like chocolate."

"I like chocolate just fine" Tina said stubbornly.

"No, no, you don't," Christine said. "That's what you tell everyone. You really don't get what's the big deal about chocolate, though. It doesn't do it for you."

"What else?" Tina asked, not admitting if Christine was telling the truth or not.

"You never know what to say to all the girls who complain about their periods. Yours is…easy, I guess," Christine said. "Or maybe not easy, but not harsh. Not like theirs."

"Go on," Tina said.

Christine's greatest love was her books. Was Tina's as

well? Or did that go beyond the body thing? Might as well try. "You love to read."

"Everybody says they like to read," Tina scoffed.

"Stanislaw Lem?" Christine challenged. "Most people haven't even heard of him."

"Who else?" Tina asked. She sounded wistful again.

"John Irving. Irving Stone." She sometimes got those two confused, but she loved them both dearly. "Lao Tsu's poetry. Walter Trevor. Andre Norton. Judith Tarr."

"Yes," Tina said slowly. "But you could know those just by looking at my bookshelf."

"What about—"

The door to the room opened slowly.

"Excuse me, Miss, it's time to get ready for the ceremony." The old butler stuck his head through the door.

He did a double-take when he saw Christine sitting there. "Ah. I *did* recognize you."

"I'm ready," Tina said, rising off the bed. "It was nice to meet you," Tina said over her shoulder as she walked to the door.

The butler smirked at Christine, then said solicitously to Tina, "I hope that old troll wasn't bothering you."

Christine couldn't hear Tina's reply. It wouldn't have mattered. Not much could sink her spirits even lower than they already were.

Then she heard the *click* of the door locking. She was stuck here, in this room.

How was she going to save Tina now? And stop the ceremony? Particularly when Tina clearly didn't want to be saved?

CHRISTINE TRIED THE DOOR ANYWAY. BUT NO, SHE'D heard correctly. It was locked. She pressed against it. Solid wood.

Was there another way out? She walked back over to the window. Fog laced the nearby trees, making the night darker. It was a long way down to the ground. Plus, there were branches in the way.

She turned and contemplated the door. She *had* to get out. Now that the butler had discovered her, was Dennis in trouble?

She quickly checked her phone. Of course, there was no reception where she was. She couldn't call Dennis and let him know he was in trouble.

Or even ask him to try to find her.

Christine knocked on the door. "Hello!" she called. She pounded louder. "I'm locked in!" she called.

No one responded. Was there anyone in the room outside? She glanced at her watch. It was still at least forty minutes before the wedding was supposed to start.

How was she going to get out of here?

She pounded on the door again. It didn't move. Could she break through the wood? *Troll out* as it were?

Christine looked at the door carefully. It opened out. The hinges were on the other side. There were six panels. The wood would be thinner, there.

Or would the side of the door, the wall, be easier to break through? Christine tapped the wall, listening for a hollow spot. Where a stud didn't hide.

People punched their way through walls all the time. Particularly guys, when they got mad enough.

Was Christine mad enough?

Lars had already started *twisting* Tina's fate. He'd convinced her that she had no magic. Taken away her power. No one should have done that.

Christine hadn't been involved for very long in non-human affairs. She still wasn't sure how she felt about the Great War.

But Lars was also a demon. And demons had broken into her home. Despoiled her reading chair.

Ruined her books.

With a growling snarl, Christine pulled back and *slammed* her fist into the wall. It gave way with a very satisfying *crunch*. When Christine looked, she saw a huge indentation where her fist had been.

Wow. She really was pissed off about things.

Two more hits, and Christine had punched a hole all the way through to the other side. It just took a little more pressing to break open the wall enough that she could reach around and open the door from the other side.

The first room was empty. The false bride and her friends had probably gone to their ceremony. The decoy. The one that most everyone, including Dennis, would be at.

Where would the second one be?

Christine knew the answer to that.

In the basement, of course. Closer to Hell.

CHRISTINE WALKED ACROSS THE OUTER ROOM, THEN pressed her ear against the door leading to the hallway. She didn't hear anything. But that didn't mean no one was out there. Just because her hearing had gotten better didn't mean demons weren't sneakier than most and able to be quiet.

She couldn't hear anyone standing just outside the door, though. And she didn't hear any footsteps approaching. Maybe no one had heard her punch her way through the wall.

Cautiously, Christine opened the door, poking her head out.

No one in sight. The hallway looked depressingly normal, actually. Family pictures hanging on the walls. Plush red carpet. Beige-colored sconces lining the walls, giving everything a soft glow.

It didn't look like a demon ceremony to change the fate of the world was about to take place.

Christine remembered coming up the hallway from her right, so she went left this time. There had to be a servant's set of stairs going down, right? That only made sense in a place as huge as this.

But Christine didn't find a second set of stairs leading down at either end of the hallway. Maybe it was hidden behind one of the closed doors she tiptoed past. She didn't want to start opening doors just to find out.

So Christine braved the front staircase. Maybe the butler was part of the ceremony and she wouldn't run into him. Hopefully the other servants were all busy, and she wouldn't run into any of them either. Or maybe she could play dumb if she did.

The wrought-iron bannister of the grand staircase was decorated with drapes of white tulle and tiny white flowers. Christine stayed close to the inside edge, walking down carefully, listening hard. Was anyone else there?

It didn't take her long to explore the second floor. Lots of closed doors, photos, even a case full of Lars' trophies from high school.

But no second staircase.

Christine went back to the main stairs again, creeping down more quiet than any mouse. As she approached the first floor, she heard servants greeting guests. More people were arriving for the wedding. No one was being directed up the stairs, though. Could she maybe blend in with one of those groups? Sneak down before anyone saw her?

Christine paused, waiting on the stairs. Sweat trickled down her back. Finally, the voices receded. She took three more steps, then crouched down, to see.

No one stood in the open front hallway.

Christine rapidly made her way down the rest of the steps, then turned to her right, going the direction she'd seen them taking Dennis, earlier.

"Oh, there you are!" A hand grabbed her elbow.

IT TOOK AT LEAST HALF A DOZEN BREATHS FOR Christine to regain her composure. "What are you doing here?" she whispered at Dennis as he walked her down the hallway.

"Looking for you," Dennis whispered back. "Come on. The ceremony is about to start."

"But this isn't the right ceremony! It's a fake," Christine told him.

They passed by two servants going the other direction, back toward the door. Christine made a point of smiling at them as if she was happy to be there, then went back to arguing with her brother.

"Tina's here! And they've done something to her memory. She didn't recognize me. Didn't remember me. Didn't remember her own Destiny," Christine told him.

"It's worse than that," Dennis said.

"How can it be worse?" Christine asked. She still had time to get out of there. Find the other ceremony. Stop the demons before they finished twisting Tina and her fate.

Dennis and Christine paused at the entrance to the huge banquet room where the fake wedding was to be held. Huge windows along the sides and at the front opened up onto more woods. A long skinny table stood against the far windows—probably an altar. Chandeliers made of glass shone with actual candles. Little bouquets of white flowers, fluffed up with more white tulle, hung everywhere.

"There," Dennis said. "Third row. On the left."

As if on cue, the couple sitting there turned to look at them.

Dennis was right. It was worse.

Mum and Dad were there.

"What are you doing here?" Christine asked as she sat down in the empty chair beside Mum. Her parents were dressed up: Dad was even wearing a conservative tie, instead of one of his cartoon ones. Mum wore a nice, dark blue dress that showed off her creamy skin—skin that Christine now knew she'd never achieve.

"The Sorgenfreys have been friends of the family for years, dear," Mum replied.

"Besides, I'd never been to their new place. Kind of swanky, huh?" Dad added.

Christine felt the familiar urge to roll her eyes at her father. He wasn't that old. Just barely fifty. But no one used words like "swanky" anymore. They hadn't used them when he'd been growing up, either.

"You shouldn't be here," Christine told them.

Her mother blinked at her. "Why would you say that?" she asked. "I know that Lars wasn't always the most polite boy to you. But boys will be boys."

Christine sighed. What on earth could she tell her parents?

"You look rather nice," Dad added.

Mum looked at Christine critically. "You really do," she added in. "That dress fits you perfectly."

Christine looked down. It was just the illusion charm, making her clothes appear to fit her like a glove.

"My little girl, all grown up," Dad said. He gave her a proud smile.

He had no idea.

A harp started playing softly. Something hymnal. The processional was going to start soon.

"If you see anything weird—anything at all—it isn't your imagination. You leave here. Run, if you can't get your car. Promise me that," Christine insisted. She couldn't protect her parents. She had to go find Tina. This was the best she could think of.

Mum and Dad looked at each other, the silent consulting that they always did.

"I'm not certain I quite understand what you're saying," Mum said, her accent coming on strongly.

Christine reached across Mum's lap and took Dad's hand. Then she gripped Mom's shoulder with her other. "I don't know what will happen. I don't know if anything will happen. If something *does* happen, you two get out of here. Promise me that."

Mum sat very still, looking shocked. Dad looked down at his hand in Christine's. "You never reach out and touch us," he commented. "What's going on?"

The music was growing louder. She had to leave.

"Promise me you'll get out of here," Christine pleaded. She had to know they'd be safe.

"Dennis?" Mum said. She leaned back so she could look at Christine's brother.

"Listen to her, Mom," Dennis said. "Do as she says."

That made Christine smile. Her brother still had her back.

"All right," Mum said slowly. "We'll leave."

"Promise?" Christine asked stubbornly.

"Promise," Dad replied. "But I still don't know what you think might happen."

"That's okay," Christine said, releasing her dad's hand, her mother's shoulder. "I don't either."

"Where are you going?" Mum asked as Christine half rose from her chair.

"I have to go," Christine told them.

"But the ceremony's just about to start!" Dad protested. "You don't want to miss it."

"I'll come back as soon as I can," Christine promised.

"I still don't know what you think will happen," Mum griped. "The Sorgenfreys are good people. This isn't about to turn into a rave or something, is it?"

No, Mum. The Sorgenfreys are actually demons. I'm not your real daughter. I need to go save your actual human daughter, stop the Great War, save the world.

"Take care of them," Christine told Dennis as she eased past him.

"I'm coming with you," Dennis told her stubbornly.

"No, you're not," Christine said. "Look. You at least have a clue," she whispered.

"I do?" Dennis teased. "That's the first time you've ever admitted that."

Christine sighed. Now was not the time for him to tease her, for their old sibling rivalry. "You have to take care of them," she ordered him. "Keep them safe. You know what we're up against."

"Yes. That's why I want to be with you," Dennis told her. "To help you."

"I'll take care of myself," Christine told him. She'd always been able to. Just had never had any confidence about it before now.

Dennis pressed his lips together before he gave a short nod. "Promise?" he asked.

"Promise," Christine told him. She gave his hand a quick squeeze.

It was a promise she intended to keep.

One of the liveried servants stepped into Christine's path as she tried to leave the event hall. She gave him a wide-eyed look and urgently whispered, "Ladies' room!"

That got the servant quickly turned around and leading Christine down a broad hallway, decorated in modern blandness. At the end of the hall stood an open door, leading to a kitchen. That didn't seem like the way down.

Christine scooted into the bathroom like she was in a hurry, then stopped.

This wasn't like a normal person's bathroom. Instead, it had two stalls and was decorated like a fancy hotel, with piles of soft towels on the counter, a wingback chair in the corner, and carpet.

Who put carpet in a bathroom? Particularly that safe shade of beige?

Christine hopped impatiently from one foot to the next before she poked her head out.

Good. Hallway was empty.

Christine hurried along as if she knew where she was going.

She kind of did. She was going to the *other* ceremony. Where Tina was to be "married." She had to stop it without changing into a troll, without her parents seeing that she was no longer their human daughter.

Christine just had to figure out where the other ceremony was.

CHAPTER TEN

Christine barely kept herself from growling in frustration as she turned back down another hallway. They were all starting to blend together: artwork, family photos, even the cases of Lars' trophies and achievements.

But no staircase leading downstairs. To the basement. To the dungeon Christine was now starting to question the existence of.

Why would anyone build a home without a basement?

Of course, not everyone was as comfortable underground as she was.

As Christine made it back toward the event hall, she heard the traditional "Here Comes the Bride" music.

Damn it. Where was the other ceremony? How was she going to stop it if she couldn't even find it?

Christine hesitated at the open door to the event hall. No groom stood at the front of the hall. The lighting seemed dimmer. Maybe the candles were just burning down.

A flash caught her eye, just outside the huge windows at the front.

Of course.

Two ceremonies.

Each in sight of the other.

One inside, tame and human and mild.

One outside, wild under the trees.

The audience would see both, witness both, perhaps. And not even realize what they were seeing.

Christine turned to go. It wouldn't be that difficult to get outside. She might even be able to go out the front door.

In the hallway, just next to the event center, was a set of doors leading out.

Red light glowed ominously through the window to the right. It had started to rain, a hissing sound, like a great cauldron.

Before Christine could open the door, an iron-like hand caught her elbow.

"Not so fast, Miss. You'll miss it all." The butler stood there, look cool and calm. As resolute as stone.

"But I just—" Christine said, trying to pull away.

"I told you I never forgot a face," the butler said confidently. "Trust me. You need to be *here*. At least for now."

"Let go of me," Christine growled. She didn't like to be touched. She *really* didn't like to be touched by demons.

"Hush," the butler hissed. Blue sparks followed the spray out of his mouth.

Christine felt her limbs go numb. She could still stand,

but it was as if she were encased in a block of ice. She could barely breathe. She couldn't move. She couldn't scream.

She was trapped.

"Now, be a good girl, and just stand there for a bit," the butler told her.

No. Christine had been a good girl for much of her life. Her human life. She was tired of it.

As a troll, she didn't have any magic. That's what Patrick had told her.

She was still going to fight this.

Christine sucked in as deep a breath as she could. Then she sucked in more air. She was bigger than this illusionary self she'd been presenting to the world. Stronger. Tougher.

Meaner.

The block of ice around her meant nothing. An inconvenience. She was going to reach out and grab that skinny butler by the throat. Shake him until what few white hairs remaining in his skull had fallen out. Grind his bones to flour, then make bread.

Christine found she could suddenly gnash her teeth. She started a low growl, deep and rumbling in her chest, trying to shake herself loose from the spell.

He could not hold her. *He would not.*

With the greatest power of will, Christine took a step forward.

Okay, maybe she only inched her right toe a little bit in front of her. But it was progress.

Christine inched the other foot ahead. Then again.

A baby could crawl faster. Hell, maybe even an ant.

But Christine would not be kept here.

Step by slow step, Christine made her way. Closer to the door. Closer to outside.

When the butler finally turned and noticed her, he couldn't hide his surprise. "My," he said, shaking his head. "You can go now. They're waiting for you."

He dismissively waved his hand. The ice around Christine fell. She could move again.

Turning quickly, Christine threw a punch at the butler's face.

He dodged it easily. "It's going to take much more than that to tackle me," he told her archly. "But you need to run along. What would the wedding ceremony with your human sister be without you?"

"If they need me, then maybe I shouldn't go. Maybe that will ruin it for them," Christine pointed out. She crossed her arms across her chest and stubbornly stayed exactly where she was.

The butler smiled at her. "Such a child. So obstinate. No. The ceremony can be completed without you. Your terror and despair will just make it all the sweeter."

A soft cry wound its way through the rain.

"I will come for you later," Christine promised.

"I know, I know. Me and all my generations," the butler said, having already turned his back and started walking away.

Another moan came on the wind.

Christine pushed her way out the doors. But she would remember the butler.

She'd made a promise. And she never broke her promises.

CHRISTINE STEPPED OUT OF THE BUILDING AND INTO a storm. Wind whipped at her skirt. Rain instantly plastered her hair to her head. It was difficult to see—not due to the dark, but the intensity of the water pouring down on her.

When Christine stepped into a puddle, she growled low in her throat. New shoes. Ruined. She could almost hear her mother's dismay.

Lars was going to pay for all of this.

The weird red lights flashed again to Christine's right. She took two steps, then hesitated. Should she go confront them as she was? Or should she *troll out?*

No. Her parents were here. She couldn't risk them seeing her.

They were going to get enough of a shock when they realized there were *two* of her.

That they'd raised the wrong daughter. That they had a different, *better* daughter now.

But if Christine wanted any answers, she was going to have to rescue Tina.

Judging by the lights, Christine headed downhill from them, slipping on the wet grass, scrambling across the dirt. She wanted to sneak back up on the ceremony, instead of blundering into it from a predictable direction.

If the butler hadn't been lying to her, they'd be expecting her.

Christine slipped and fell as she started in under the trees. Her palms stung and her hip hurt. Now, her dress was ruined, too. She was really going to kill Lars. Or at least do him some bodily damage.

The flashing red lights remained to Christine's right. She circled around until they were behind her, then pushed her way through the trees, falling again. The mud was wet and cold. At least it smelled clean. She was a complete mess.

Christine hid behind a tree, then sneaked to the next, trying to stay out of sight. The lights flashed brighter. What were they doing? She couldn't hear any moans or cries, now.

Finally, Christine got close enough to see. It was a large open area, maybe forty feet across. Lars stood with his back to the house, on the far side. He wore a long red robe over his formal tux and tails.

Bastard was also standing under a huge awning. Wasn't wet.

Behind him stood his parents. Another surge of anger flowed through Christine. While her own mother was pretty, Lars' mother was Stepford-wife perfect. The kind of beauty that was only achieved through millions in surgery and demon magic, with blonde hair and blue eyes and a killer black gown that sparkled in the dim light. Lars' father had the kind of rugged good looks that would inspire thousands to follow him and go to war.

Two priests stood on either side, dressed also in long robes. They were obviously demons, with elongated faces and snake-like snouts. Slits for pupils. Red, black, and white scales covered their faces, their arms.

Was that…blood? Dripping from their clawed fingertips? They passed a chalice from one to the other, dipping their fingers in whatever the hell that red liquid was and anointing each other's foreheads.

Ugh.

Just in front of Christine, barely visible through the trees, Tina knelt on the ground. She wasn't under an umbrella. The muslin shift had been plastered to her skin by the rain. Her blonde hair hung down in wet strings.

Ropes kept Tina's arms spread out wide. She appeared unhurt. Maybe it wasn't her blood the priests were using.

Christine longed for a knife. Something that she could use to cut Tina's bonds with. The rope looked thick and strong, like the kind used in gym class.

The knots were also big and thick. Shouldn't be too hard to untie them. If she could only sneak up invisibly.

Maybe Tina would believe her now.

Christine took a step forward. She didn't have much of a plan. Rush in and throw the cup of blood all over the priests. Like some kind of PETA protest. See if that would ruin the ceremony.

Strong arms caught hers.

Damn it! The demons on either side of her hadn't been there a moment ago, she would have sworn it.

"Yoo-hoo!" Lars called out.

Christine struggled against the demons holding her. She couldn't break free. They were stronger than she was.

Against her will, the demons dragged Christine forward. Forced her to her knees beside Tina.

"You said you were going to marry me," Tina moaned. She was still enspelled.

"Look what the cat dragged in," Lars said, shaking his head.

Christina glanced down. She was a mess. Soaking wet. Covered in mud. Scratched by trees and demon claws.

She looked up, bared her teeth and growled. Didn't matter what her appearance was. She was still going to fight him. Tooth and claw and fang.

"Now with both of you, the war will go on forever," Lars gloated. His eyes gleamed red.

"Her fate was to end the war, wasn't it?" Christine asked. "Her Destiny."

Lars nodded. "After the ceremony, the Great War will never end. It shall be Hell on earth. And we will rule forever."

"No," Christine said, automatically denying it. "The tide will turn. Another Great War will arise. Nothing stays the same forever." She knew that, now. Down into her bones.

Nothing stayed the same. Not even her.

"Too bad you won't be here to cheer them on," Lars said, not sounding sorry at all.

He stepped back, and the priests started their ceremony again.

There *had* to be a way for Christine to break out of this. To break the demons' hold. They held arms that only looked human.

She'd noticed before that when she wore the illusion, she wasn't at her full troll strength. She needed to transform. To *troll out*.

She moaned and swayed forward, as if defeated. The demons tightened their grips on her upper arms.

Neither of them held her hands.

Christine leaned a bit more forward. Her necklace

hung down, outside her dress. With an abrupt jerk, she slid her right hand around it.

The demon yanked her arm back, helping her break the chain.

With a great shake, Christine shook the rest of the spell from her. Her skin grew green and mottled. Muscles popped up along her arms. Fangs sprouted from her upper and lower jaws. Claws formed at the ends of her hands.

The demons on either side of her gasped and loosened their grip.

Christine roared and surged to her feet, slashing at the demon to her left. He let go in surprise and fell back. She tried to claw at the demon still holding her on her right. He stepped out of the way but didn't let go.

The priests continued their droning. They weren't about to let a little thing like a fight interrupt their ceremony.

Christine grabbed hold of the wrist of the demon holding her, then pivoted to the left, throwing him off his feet. He let go as he fell, but scrambled back up again, lunging for Christine. He tackled her and they both fell into the mud.

The other demon had abandoned the fight and gone to hold Tina's throat back. Both priests had drawn long knives out of their robes—glinting cold steel. They were both blessing it. Lars' parents stood with their eyes closed, holding hands and chanting. Lars had his arms open, as if welcoming his bride-to-be.

A whirlwind started in the open space between where Lars and the priests stood and Christine fought. Sickly yellow light spilled over from it. The stench of rotten eggs and moldy water rose above the smell of the mud.

They were opening a portal to Hell. To bring it here.

Christine threw the demon off her. Then stomped on its face. A satisfying *crunch* of bones sounded under her heel. Then she attacked the demon holding Tina, throwing it against a tree. It landed *hard*, lying curled around the roots. Motionless.

She threw herself at Tina, wrapping one arm around the girl while slashing at the ropes with her claws.

"I remember you, now," Tina said, struggling to get away from Christine. "You were the one who brought the demons to our house."

"No! I didn't!" Christine said, horrified. "Why would I be fighting them if I was helping them?"

"You're not human," Tina said, still fighting her.

"I'm here to save your life," Christine growled, finally freeing one of the girl's arms. "If you'd just listen to me!"

"I have to end the war," Tina said. She stopped trying to pull away from Christine and reached up to help with the other rope.

"Yes. Exactly," Christine said. Finally, she was getting through to the girl.

A sharp blow to Christine's back let her know that one of the demons had recuperated. She let go of Tina and turned to face it.

She gulped. Them. Both demons growled at her. One slashed forward and clawed Christine's arm. She howled in pain, and let go of Tina.

"By marrying Lars!" Tina finished freeing herself and jumped away. Heading straight into the maelstrom that was building in the center of the clearing. Tina was now covered in that sickly yellow light, held there, like a fly in a spider's web. Lars laughed as the rain pelted down harder. His eyes glowed red and he grew taller.

How could Christine stop him? She howled a second and third time, giving vent to her anger and frustration. She'd grown up *wrong* because of him. Stolen from her bio-parents. Her future.

He was *not* going to win.

Using all of her inhuman strength, Christine wheeled and threw the hardest punch she could at the first demon. Her fist hit his face. *Crunch.* She brought her foot up and kicked the second demon in the stomach, sending it flying through the trees a second time. Damn thing should just stay down.

She couldn't get Tina free of the sticky magic. That would take a different kind of strength.

Instead, Christine ran around the storm.

Directly at Lars.

"You would dare to challenge me?" Lars asked. His voice had grown deeper. More demonic. He calmly dodged Christine's attack. He was still mostly human. Just bigger. Darker. Scalier.

"She ain't the only one," came a loud voice from behind Lars.

"What—" was all Lars got out. Distracted, he didn't move quickly enough this time.

Christine's fist sank into his stomach. Lars doubled over.

Dennis stood behind Lars. He gave him a sharp kick.

Lars suddenly *moved* in a way that was distinctly not

human. So fast she could barely track his progress. To the side, then back. So he was no longer between them.

Christine would have been impressed if Lars hadn't moved behind Dennis, then grabbed him by the throat. Showing off, of course, lifting him up with a single hand.

"No, you don't," Christine growled. She tore into Lars. Reached beyond her struggling brother. Slashed Lars' chest with her claws. Took hold of his other arm. Found how satisfying it was to use her tusks to bite.

Howling, Lars dropped Dennis , who crawled rapidly away, out of harm's reach. If only he would keep crawling. Would leave. Like he'd promised. Hadn't he promised her to go?

Lars turned angrily to Christine. "You don't know what you're doing."

"Neither do you," Christine shot back. "Even if you brought Hell to earth, who says the demons from there would thank you? Or my people?"

"We were meant to rule you," Lars said.

"Not anymore," Christine told him.

Lars struck out at Christine, enraged.

He was fast. Inhumanly fast.

Christine still dodged the blow. She wasn't human, either.

Howls erupted from all sides. Just beyond Lars, guests poured out through the grand doors of the event hall.

And started transforming. Orcs. Trolls. Goblins. Dwarves. Strange purple-eyed Japanese spirits. There were even fairer creatures—elves and fairies and sprites.

The demons behind Christine now howled. They surged toward the others. Started fighting.

Christine lunged forward, grappling with Lars. She held his arms and dug her claws in. He did the same. She snapped at him. He didn't have the bite she did.

"You won't win!" Lars told her.

At least he was now getting wet. Christine tried to kick him.

"Your other self is lost!" he claimed.

Christine swung them around.

Tina still stood in the middle of the sickly yellow light, twitching. Her eyes were nearly dead. She was being drained. She couldn't get out.

Christine tried to let go of Lars. To get away. To save her human sister.

Lars laughed and hung on.

"May I cut in?" came a very polite voice from the side.

Christine whirled to find Patrick standing beside her. He was dressed in a formal suit. Just his head had transformed, showing his true orcish nature. He gave a swift, effective punch to Lars' jaw.

"But you don't believe in violence!" Christine said as she stumbled back, suddenly freed from Lars' grip.

"I don't believe in assholes winning, either," Patrick told her. He turned back to Lars and growled. "Now, come pick on someone your own size. If you dare."

"Thanks!" Christine shouted as she raced away.

Toward Tina. Her human sister. That other part of her.

"Tina! Tina!" Christine shouted just at the edge

of the light. She didn't want to touch it. Didn't want to get caught in it. It oozed around Tina's body. Sucked her spirit away.

Tina looked up. Her eyes were glassed over. Hazy. "He said he would marry me," she moaned.

"Would you forget about him?" Christine snapped. "You need to shake yourself out of this. *You're* the one who's important. *You're* the one with a Destiny. Not him."

"But you're a troll! Why would you care?" Tina asked.

"Because I'm a changeling," Christine told her. "I took your place in the human world. So you could train. Have magic. Be…important."

Tina gasped and sagged as the light wrapped more tightly around her.

"Reach your hand out!" Christine told her. "Give me something to grab onto!"

"I can't!" Tina said.

"You damned well better," Christine growled. "You will *not* make my life a waste."

Tina struggled feebly.

She wasn't going to get out. Not before being sucked dry.

Damn it. Christine's whole life was just about being a stand-in for someone else, wasn't it?

With one last frustrated howl, Christine plunged forward. She tried to run as fast as she could. She tackled Tina around the waist, attempting to throw her out of the light.

Planning on taking her place instead.

Cold and cold and cold. That was all Christine could think. Feel. Breathe. That cold had invaded even her bones. The light blinded her. She could barely see.

She hadn't succeeded, however. Tina was still there. Trapped. Like two flies in sickly honey. Wrapped around each other like conjoined twins.

"I remember you," Tina whispered, the words falling onto Christine's head from above.

Christine's thighs ached, but she couldn't straighten her legs from her awkward position. Her arms trembling with holding on. Still, she pushed. Up. Out.

To her surprise, Christine found herself standing up straighter. Still holding onto Tina.

"I have a Destiny," Tina whispered.

Christine nodded. She did. She was important.

"So do you," Tina added.

The surprise was almost enough for Christine to pull back. Not strong enough to break the spell holding them.

"To save you," Christine finally guessed when Tina stopped whispering.

"To save the world," Tina told her.

"I'm a nobody," Christine said. "A troll." Not even human.

"So?" Tina asked. "Only you have the strength to push us away from here."

Christine would have shaken her head if she could. She didn't have the strength to fight this. No one did.

"I'll help," Tina said. She breathed hot air down Christine's back. Across her shoulder.

The ice didn't melt. But it reminded Christine that

there was a sun. Even if she didn't like it very much. It was there.

And she was going to see it again.

Inch by glacial inch, Christine fought to get them out of the trap. Out of the ice that formed in her veins. To move. To change. To be different. Even if that meant being a troll.

Did it take hours? Days? Seconds? It was impossible for Christine to judge her progress. But she inched along. Bringing them to the edge. She sensed the fighting just beyond. It wouldn't take much. But she was exhausted. Drained.

"Just a little more," Tina whispered. "Then we're home. Free. A hot-tub and two-book night."

Christine nearly laughed. That was her greatest indulgence—to spend an entire evening in the bathtub, with two water-stained books to keep her company. To keep filling up the tub with hot water as she read. She wouldn't finish either of them, just dip into one then the other as her mood dictated.

It buoyed her up. That promise of comfort. A good read. Her old friends.

Christine broke them out of the magical light.

A whirlwind battle raged around them. It was impossible to tell who was winning.

"You can put me down, now."

Christine belatedly realized that she still held Tina. "Sorry," she said gruffly, bending stiffly to place her human sister on the ground.

"Thank you," Tina said. Then Tina turned toward the light. It still oozed. It was much larger than it had been.

The portal was still going to open.

Tina frowned. Held up both hands, palms out. "No," she said. Quietly. Distinctly. "No."

That was it. The light started to shrink, abashed, as if it had been caught doing something naughty.

"No," Tina said again.

The light seeped away faster now. The portal slammed closed.

The fighting around them died down in ripples as the demons discovered they'd lost.

Tina pointed across the clearing at Lars and his family. "Arrest these men," she said in clear, bell-like tones.

Patrick gave Lars a good clobber on his head, dropping him to his knees. "Begging the lady's pardon, but we're not police officers."

Tina sniffed. "Citizen's arrest will do. They kidnapped me and held me against my will for a week."

"Yes, ma'am," Patrick said. He grabbed Lars and brought him back up to his feet. "We'll take him to the court of the Host for holding."

"Thank you," Tina said.

Even Christine was dazzled by the brightness of her smile.

"Christine! Are you all right?"

Just beyond where Patrick was force-marching Lars away stood Mum and Dad.

Christine braced herself for the worst. Mum and Dad started to rush over. Dennis was a few feet behind them. It looked as though he'd gone a few rounds with some demons himself.

As Christine expected, Mum and Dad were going straight for Tina.

But no. They veered. Came to her, instead.

"Dear, you're bleeding!" Mum said looking at Christine's arm, all scratched and gouged from her fight with the demons, from where Lars had dug his claws in.

It hadn't really hurt until now that she was thinking about it.

"But, but, how do you recognize me?" Christine asked. Her parents hadn't known she was a troll all along, had they?

"I told them," Dennis confessed. "When the battle started."

Christine looked from Mum to Dad to Mum again. They had brave smiles pasted on their faces. Determined to do the right thing.

"It's okay," Christine said. Her heart ached more than her wounds. "She's really your daughter," she added, indicating Tina.

Mum and Dad turned and looked critically at Tina. She waved at them, hesitant.

"She looks an awful lot like the girl we raised," Mum admitted. "And we'd like to get to meet her. To know her. But she's a stranger. You're our daughter."

"But I'm not human!" Christine said, feeling as though she had to state the obvious.

"Explains a lot, actually, Sis," Dennis teased.

"We can formally adopt you," Dad said. "Promise to always keep you."

Dad wasn't magic. He and Mum were one hundred percent mundane. Still, the way he spoke, and the word *promise*, that word that had always been so important to their family, held a resonance that Christine hadn't expected.

"I would have thought you'd be freaking out more," Christine said, not agreeing, not yet.

"There was freaking," Dad said, nodding. "And there will be more. But you're still our stubborn, recalcitrant, wonderful daughter. No matter what shape you're in."

Christine swallowed hard around the sudden lump in her throat.

Maybe she did still have a family after all.

CHAPTER ELEVEN

CHRISTINE PERCHED UNCOMFORTABLY ON THE EDGE of the beige and red striped sofa in Tina's parents' living room. Tina sat beside her. Christine wished she could get a picture taken of the pair of them, both human, the light and dark version.

Mrs. Zimmerman sat opposite them, on a matching chair, looking as uncomfortable as Christine felt. The room was nice enough, photos and art covering the walls, a thick green carpet on the floor, and stylish, modern wooden furniture filling every space.

It was similar to what Christine had grown up with. Though her mum had more antiques—like the porcelain tea set from Grandma.

The Zimmermans themselves were quite ordinary looking. Both were white, dressed in cardigans and jeans, nice shirts and good shoes. They weren't rich. They didn't look magical, though Tina had assured Christine that they were both quite powerful spell casters.

Christine didn't see any evidence of that just looking at them.

Mr. Zimmerman came back in the room. Handed a sheaf of papers to Christine. "You'll find everything there," he said quietly. He sat down on the ottoman next to his wife. Took her hand.

"It's all quite legal," Mrs. Zimmerman insisted. "That we adopted you."

Except they hadn't. They'd merely passed her along. Stolen Tina.

The papers supported the story that the Zimmermans told Christine: she'd been given up for adoption by her birth mother.

With these papers, however, it was possible that Christine could find her parents.

"Thank you," Christine said, standing.

"I'm sorry we couldn't be of more help," Mr. Zimmerman said slowly as he stood.

Christine shrugged. At least they'd kept the original papers. It gave her a place to start.

"Come on," Tina said, also standing.

"Where are you going?" Mrs. Zimmerman asked. An edge of fear colored her question.

"With Christine. To see if we can find her parents," Tina explained evenly.

"Are you sure that's wise?" Mr. Zimmerman asked. He also looked worried. "No offense," he said hurriedly to Christine. "It's just that—we don't know you. And we're not used to you just…going," he added, turning to Tina.

It was Tina's turn to shrug. "It's safe. Well, *safer*," she hastily added before her mother could object. "All those demons are still being held by the Host. There's enough evidence that they've been willfully blinding the system, as well as twisting the law, that they won't get out for a very, very long time."

Christine smiled at that. Ty *had* found evidence of demons tampering with reality in ways that were one hundred percent illegal. Blocking the International District gate had also been considered a serious offense.

Lars and his family would be gone for a long, long time.

"The oracles haven't made their proclamation yet," Tina added.

Christine tried to contain her wince. Since she'd touched Tina, broken the changeling spell, Tina's original Destiny had started changing. No one knew if she was still destined to stop the Great War or if the opportunity had passed by.

"And Christine wouldn't let anything happen to me," Tina concluded.

"That's correct," Christine said, leveling a hard look at both the Zimmermans. "I'll protect her." She paused, took a breath, then swallowed. "I promise."

The words had a solemn quality that Christine hadn't intended. Perhaps because the room was magically protected in some way and the promise took on more weight.

The couple looked impressed at that. "I see," Mr. Zimmerman said slowly. "Thank you."

What had just happened? Had Christine just re-bound them together again? She followed Tina out of the house.

"Well, that was—" Christine started to say.

"Not here," Tina said. She outlined a door with rough gestures of one hand. A portal appeared. Tina stepped through immediately.

With a sigh, Christine followed her. Now what?

They ended up in a park that Christine wasn't familiar with. The sweet smell of pines surrounded them. To her right, Christine saw the curve of a lake.

Tina sketched another doorway. Stepped through.

After three more stops, Tina finally brought them to Christine's apartment. "They won't be able to follow *that* trail," she said smugly as she waited for Christine to open the door.

Why was Tina trying to hide her path? It wasn't as if it wouldn't be that difficult to locate Christine.

"Let's find out who your bio-parents are," Tina announced as she marched into the living room. She folded her legs and sank gracefully to the floor. From some hidden pocket in the air she pulled out a large pink-plastic container, about two feet square.

"Okay," Christine said slowly. She was really going to have to ask how Tina did that. Being able to store books that way, and then retrieve them from anywhere, would be awesome.

At Tina's gesture, Christine sank down to the floor opposite her.

Her bookshelves were only half full, now. No books lay in cozy piles on the floor. At least everything had been cleaned, the spray paint removed. A new chair, as comfortable as her old one, sat in the corner.

She hadn't refinished the shelves, not yet. She kept putting it off. On the one hand, the scars disturbed her, reminded her of that awful time. On the other hand, they were kind of like battle scars. Her own skin had completely healed.

Tina took the papers from Christine and placed the adoption paper in the center between them. She pulled two glowing white crystals, each the size of Christine's troll fist, from the plastic container and also set them on the ground. Then she pulled out what looked like a human magician's wand, black with a white tip.

"Really?" Christine asked. That was what Tina used?

Tina shrugged. "Habit," she said. She drew bright circles around the paper lying on the floor while muttering in that language that Christine still thought she should know.

The light gathered itself together into a glowing purple ball. It pulled light and energy from Tina, from Christine, from the two crystals into itself.

"Good," Tina said, nodding. "When the spell expires, the image of your birth mother should appear right there."

The ball rose and grew. It hummed softly, but not in an annoying way. The purple turned brighter.

When it reached head height, it started fading, from purple to a softer lavender.

Then it faded away into nothing. No light remained. No picture appeared. The strong scent of rosemary filled the room.

"Dang it! That wasn't what was supposed to happen," Tina said.

"Why didn't it work?" Christine asked.

Tina bit her lips thoughtfully. "I wonder if the records are magically sealed."

Christine nodded. She tried not to show her own disappointment. While it was wonderful that her human family still wanted her, she'd hoped that maybe her troll family did as well.

"Maybe you could get a court order to unseal the records," Tina said slowly.

Christine shrugged. "If they wanted to know me, they wouldn't have hidden my birth." She tried not to be bitter. But she still had a sour taste in her mouth, like plain yogurt gone stale.

"I'll ask my teachers," Tina promised Christine as she picked the crystals up and put them back into the bright pink-plastic box. "Maybe there's a better spell I could use. Get at least a hint."

"Thanks," Christine said politely. But she knew there wasn't one. Tina had been taught magic by the finest teachers available. Chances were that she'd already used the best spell possible.

"So do you want to go out sometime?" Tina asked all in a rush as she stood up. "You know. Try some wine or beer or something?"

"Wasn't that how we got into all this mess in the first place?" Christine asked, bemused. Not like she was interested in going out to a bar.

"Yes, but I really want to be able to go out sometimes," Tina said. "And my parents like you."

"No, they don't," Christine said. They could barely wait for her to leave.

"Okay. So maybe they don't. But I don't care," Tina said stubbornly. "I still think it's a raw deal you got. At least they told me about my bio-parents."

"Really?" Christine asked. She was curious how that had all worked.

Tina sighed. "Not when I was a kid, no. They didn't tell me I was adopted until I was twenty-one. Then I was told I couldn't meet my bio-parents, couldn't seek them out, could never talk to them. There was too much danger, all the time." She took a deep breath. "That's when I learned about you, too."

Christine nodded. It made sense that they wouldn't tell a super-powerful magical being about her background until she was old enough to not go seek them in a teenaged huff.

"But I think the danger isn't as bad, now. And I'd still like to go out," Tina continued.

"People would mistake us for sisters," Christine told her slowly.

Tina nodded, a mischievous smile glinting that Christine didn't recognize from her own reflection in the mirror. "Twins," she said. "And we have the same tastes. No place too loud. And nothing too alcoholic or nasty tasting. We could try that new cider bar. Just down the hill."

"All right," Christine said. She thought for a moment. "Next Friday? Meet here at eight?"

"It's a deal," Tina said. "Thank you."

"For what?" Christine asked. She hadn't really done anything. Except agree to go out and probably do something she'd end up hating.

"For trying. For not being too weird about the whole changeling thing. For still wanting to hang out with me," Tina said. "I didn't have any brothers or sisters. Or a lot of friends. I wasn't ever able to go out and do much. It was always just a lot of work."

"Okay," Christine said. Could a changeling and her doppelganger be friends?

She was willing to try.

"And she can't find out who your birth mom is?" Dennis asked over dinner the next day. He said he owed her for saving the world or something. Christine hadn't ever been to this restaurant. It was on Broadway, fancy, with heavy silverware and plates rimmed with gold. She knew which fork to use of the three that graced the side of her setting. She was still concerned about accidentally crushing something.

The dress she'd worn to the wedding had been ruined. But she'd found another at the back of her closet, gray and sleek, that fit her better, now. Dennis wasn't in a suit, but he did have on a good shirt and slacks.

"Maybe I can go to court to get the records unsealed," Christine told him. "But that's a long shot."

"Do you really want to know?" Dennis said. He wouldn't meet her eye.

"I'm curious," Christine admitted. And she was. She probably always would be. "But you know that you're my family, right?"

"Yeah," Dennis said. He finally looked up at her. "It was kind of awesome, watching you fight. And…kind of different."

Was he scared? Had she actually frightened her brother?

"Don't worry. I won't bite you," she teased. She couldn't ever fight him physically in her native state—he was too vulnerable, as a human. She really was in a better position, now, to take care of him.

Dennis gave an exaggerated shudder. "I'd tell you to go see a dentist about that overbite, but I think it's natural."

Christine giggled. "I think you're right," she said. "All the better to protect you, my dear."

Dennis gave a slow nod. "You know, I think Mum was right. You are ready. Aren't you?"

Christine nodded. "There's still a lot for me to figure out," she warned. "But yeah. I'm going to be okay, now."

And she was.

CHRISTINE WENT TO SEE NIKOLAI THE NEXT NIGHT. The Chinese gate to the International District was open at least. It made her grin. Thwarting Lars and the demons gave her great joy.

The abandoned building where Nikolai kept his shop looked as desolate as always. More graffiti had been added to the plywood covering what had once been a graceful door. Christine could almost see what had been there.

Just approaching the doorway set the portal in motion. Blue and swirling. Christine wished Dennis would be able to see it sometime.

If Tina had magic and power, did Dennis? Christine

would have to be sure to ask her when they went out. Dennis would probably find that really cool.

Had he been a bit frightened of her? When she'd been fighting? Christine hadn't held anything back. She knew better than to ask him. He'd never admit it.

The shop looked much the same as it always had. Low shelves filling the center of the tall-ceilinged room. The spicy smell of dried sage, cumin, rosemary, and other herbs. This time, Christine felt her skin prickle as she passed by the shelves with the magical kits. Was she starting to sense magic?

Nikolai came around the counter, both hands out. "I hear we owe you a debt, for preventing an endless war," he said.

Christine hesitantly took his wooden hands in hers. They didn't feel human, though they were still warm. Strong. Smooth. "You're welcome," she said awkwardly.

At his prompting tug, Christine bent over so the little wooden shopkeeper could kiss both her cheeks. His lips didn't move. But he still made a kissing sound.

"So how can I help you this evening?" Nikolai asked, stepping back. His plain, painted black eyes twinkled with humor.

"I know it's only been a week or so," Christine said, hesitant. "But I wanted you to double check my illusion charm." She knew she'd been pushing against it, stressing the magic.

"But of course!" Nikolai said.

Christine took off the charm. Shook herself. Shook the illusion off.

Nikolai looked puzzled. "Why did you do that?"

"To get rid of the last of the magic," Christine explained. Didn't she have to do that?

"Just taking off the charm should break the illusion," Nikolai explained. He reached behind the counter and grabbed what looked like a magnifying glass, however, very ornate. Gold scrollwork held the lens, and the handle was made of mother-of-pearl. Examined the charm carefully.

"This charm is dead," Nikolai said after another long moment. "Drained. It's so cold I'd say it probably happened a few days ago."

"That's not possible," Christine said. "It's been working fine all week." She'd been wearing the illusion of her human body the entire time.

"No, no," Nikolai said. He smiled at her. "You've been powering the illusion. Not this."

"I can't do magic!" Christine told him. Tina had to have training in order to use hers.

Nikolai dug behind the counter again, emerging this time with a pair of goggles that fit perfectly over his painted eyes. "Here," he said, handing Christine the charm. "Do what you normally do."

Christine took the charm, put it over her neck. Then she held out her hands and watched them change from green and clawed to smaller, human, pink.

"You're doing that work," Nikolai announced. "The charm is a talisman for you. Part of a magical ritual. But you're powering it."

"But trolls aren't magical!" Christine said, shocked. How could she have been doing magic?

"You're right. Most trolls aren't," Nikolai said slowly.

"But some are. Some are *very* magical." He paused, thinking. "Did you make that charm? From the kit?"

Christine nodded. "But it kept setting so quickly! I couldn't really form it into anything." That was why she hadn't brought it into the shop—it was just an ugly lump of dough.

"Let me guess—it froze up when you tried stirring the crystals," Nikolai said.

"Yes," Christine admitted.

"That's because those crystals are magic. They react to magic. Because *you* are a magical creature, you only needed a pinch of them. Not the full amount."

"Oh," was all Christine had to say.

She was magical?

"You said you're a changeling, right?" Nikolai asked. "Do you know who your parents are?"

Christine shook her head. "And when Tina tried to do a divination spell, it didn't work. The records are sealed."

Nikolai rocked back and forth on his feet, from heel to toe. The boards creaked in an odd manner. "This Tina. She's your human doppelganger, right?"

"Yes." Christine still wasn't sure how she felt about that.

"Is it possible her family stole you?" Nikolai asked.

Christine shrugged. "Her parents said it was an adoption. They gave me the paperwork."

Nikolai snorted. "Of course they'd say that. And it might have been. However…" He paused. Sighed. "All the trolls who are magical? Particularly *your* level of magical? Are royalty."

"Royalty?" Christine asked. She snorted. "Are you kidding me?"

"No. Not at all," Nikolai said. "So maybe the humans aren't lying. Maybe it was an adoption. And maybe the records *are* sealed. But for reasons other than you'd think. It was because your mother was part of the royal family. A princess, perhaps."

Christine opened her mouth, then shut it again without saying anything.

She was magical?

Patrick had kind of hinted at that. She'd explained it away, however, as part of living under an enchantment her entire life.

"You should find out for certain," Nikolai said seriously. "Who your birth parents are."

"Why?" Christine asked, her ready temper flaring. "If they wanted me to find them, they wouldn't have blocked my origins. So that a divination could be used to discover them."

Nikolai tapped his wooden fingers on the counter for a few moments while he thought. "It was this Tina who did the divination for you. Yes?"

"Yes," Christine admitted.

"You should find someone else to do it. Someone who's reputable. Who doesn't have an interest in keeping you in the dark," Nikolai said.

"But I trust Tina," Christine pointed out.

"And maybe that's your first problem," Nikolai said. "Never trust a human."

Christine walked out of the shop with Nikolai's words still ringing in her ears. *Never trust a human.* Did he believe that because he was…whatever race or magical creature that he was? Or was he right?

It had never sat well with Christine that Tina's family had just stolen the human version of her. Fostered a troll into her family.

Dennis. Mum. And Dad. They were her family. Despite being human. She could trust them, couldn't she?

But Tina? Christine was determined to be more careful around her and her family.

Christine might be able to trust humans. Some humans. But her doppelganger? That had yet to be determined.

CHRISTINE HAD HER ILLUSION SELF FIRMLY IN PLACE. She still couldn't believe that she'd been doing the magic, creating the illusion without the charm. However, she'd tried it one night. Put the charm on her dresser. Then changed forms. Back and forth. Without touching it.

How was she the one doing it? Making her body and what she wore look so much better than it ever had before? Looking like she'd always wanted to look?

But she was. And she was going to give herself credit for it as well.

Christine still wore the necklace. It was a good reminder to her. To stay human. Because without it, she was afraid she'd *troll out* someday. For no good reason, other than someone was late returning some of the archives' papers, or perhaps even accidentally ripping something important.

There were days she felt particularly trollish.

But today, she was off to do her first community service hours. Working at a food bank, in northern Seattle.

The size of the organization surprised her. Were there that many of her kind in the community who needed help? The quick tour of the facility left her dizzy. There was a walk-in freezer the size of her living room. A walk-in fridge twice as big. Aisles were stacked with dry goods. The front, where the clients would come, had two long lines of tables, all full of goods. Some of it "normal"—Ramen noodles and cans of soup and eggs and boxes of wilted lettuce.

Some of it wasn't. Ground-up glass. Bundles of twigs. Long coiled plastic springs. Piles of shaved metal.

After additional instructions on what to do, how to hand out the cans of soup in front of her, how many based on the numbers each person in line would have, there was a lull. Christine took a deep breath. Outside stood a long line of beings. Mostly human. Some only half-human. Half something else.

"Hi," came a soft voice from beside her.

Christine turned to look. "Sorry!" she said. "I'm Christine," she added, holding out a hand.

The cute young man standing beside her said, "I'm Joe." He wore a plain gray T-shirt over a muscled chest, jeans, and sneakers. His blond-brown hair curled a little on the edges, flaring out.

He flashed her a smile that suddenly contained tusks, then just as suddenly, went back to fully human.

Troll tusks.

"I'm very new here," Christine confided.

"I'll keep an eye out for you," Joe said. "I've been coming here for three years, now."

"Volunteering?" Christine asked.

Joe shrugged. "Was in trouble, once. On that side of the line," he added, nodding toward the middle, where the clients would be coming shortly. "Got a good job now. Work in marketing. Never going back."

"I'm here for court-ordered community service," Christine admitted.

"I knew I liked you. Little law-breaker," Joe teased.

Could she flash him a tusky grin? Never would know unless she tried.

Christine tried. Joe gasped.

"I'm very pleased to meet you," Joe said warmly. "We'll have to grab coffee after our shift."

"I'm here with my brother," Christine warned.

"The human?" Joe asked. At Christine's nod, he added, "I really want to hear all about it, then. And all about you."

"Only if you'll tell me your story as well," Christine insisted.

"Deal," Joe said. A deep ringing bell sounded. The door opened. Beings poured in.

It was loud. Chaotic. Crowded. Too many people demanding too many things, all at once. Christine didn't contain her growl.

"It'll be okay," Joe said softly. "You got this."

Christine felt herself taking a deep breath.

Joe was right.

She could do this.

She could do anything, now.

READ MORE!

Be sure to read all the books in the Seattle Trolls series!

The Changeling Troll
The Princess Troll
The Fairy-Bridge Troll
The Troll-Demon War
The Troll-Human War
The Troll-Troll War

Available for sale now!

ABOUT THE AUTHOR

Leah Cutter writes page-turning fiction in exotic locations, such as a magical New Orleans, the ancient Orient, Hungary, the Oregon coast, rural Kentucky, Seattle, Minneapolis, and many others.

She writes literary, fantasy, mystery, science fiction, and horror fiction. Her short fiction has been published in magazines like *Alfred Hitchcock's Mystery Magazine* and *Talebones*, anthologies like Fiction River, and on the web. Her long fiction has been published both by New York publishers as well as small presses.

Find Leah's books here.

Follow her blog at www.LeahCutter.com.

Reviews

It's true. Reviews help me sell more books. If you've enjoyed this story, please consider leaving a review of it on your favorite site.

Come someplace new…

Are you a traveler? Do you enjoy exploring strange new worlds, new cultures, new people?

Sign up for my newsletter and I'll start you on your travels with a free copy of my book, *The Island Sampler.*

I will never spam you or use your email for nefarious purposes. You can also unsubscribe at any time.

http://www.LeahCutter.com/newsletter/

ABOUT KNOTTED ROAD PRESS

Knotted Road Press fiction specializes in dynamic writing set in mysterious, exotic locations.

Knotted Road Press non-fiction publishes autobiographies, business books, cookbooks, and how-to books with unique voices.

Knotted Road Press creates DRM-free ebooks as well as high-quality print books for readers around the world.

With authors in a variety of genres including literary, poetry, mystery, fantasy, and science fiction, Knotted Road Press has something for everyone.

Knotted Road Press
www.KnottedRoadPress.com

www.ingramcontent.com/pod-product-compliance
Lightning Source LLC
Chambersburg PA
CBHW070640100726
47907CB00007B/2050